Attaining Zero

Attaining Zero

By

Michael Flynn

Blackie & Co
Publishers Ltd

A BLACKIE & CO PUBLISHERS PAPERBACK

© Copyright 2002
M Flynn

The right of M Flynn to be identified as the author of this work has been asserted by him in accordance with the Copyright, Designs and Patents Act 1988

All Rights Reserved
No reproduction, copy or transmission of this publication may be made without written permission.
No paragraph of this publication may be reproduced, copied or transmitted save with the written permission or in accordance with the provisions of the Copyright Act 1956 (as amended).
Any person who does any unauthorised act in relation to this publication may be liable to criminal prosecution and civil claims for damage.

First published in 2002

A CIP catalogue record for this title is available from the British Library

ISBN 1 903138 38 8

**Blackie & Co Publishers Ltd
107-111 Fleet Street
LONDON EC4A 2AB**

Cover design by Pete Lamern
Casual Photographer, Part Time Guitarist
Full Time Friend.

FOREWORD
By Hannah C. Beaumont

When I close my eyes in bed I can hear a sound, that familiar click-clicking of fingers going ten to the dozen on the computer keyboard at the foot of the bed. I can smell the cigarette smoke rising and I note the little pauses in the clicking whilst he sips his tea. This makes me smile because I know that Mick is truly happy writing, he wanders off into his own little world of words and when he returns I know he will enthusiastically tell me where he has been. These are the sounds of a writer shaping his work, and these are the sounds I've heard – a patient dedicated sound, the sounds that created the book you're about to read.

Honesty is a virtue because it creates stability, and it means a lot when someone is honest with you, it's the knowing of someone in and out (warts and all). This is the canvas on which Mick writes. We're not perfect, but not many of us admit it, not many of us want to laugh at our mistakes and just start again.

When I first met Mick he was trying to come to terms with a lot of things, and many times I think he was more than willing to let these 'demons' crawl all over him. I proof-read the book for him and there were parts that made me cry because I was there and I couldn't stop him feeling how he did, but even in the darkest times he found the humour inside. This humour has been his saving grace, his ability to laugh at disaster has got me through. By us I mean all of us, him, you, them, me. It's a fantastic thing to be able to do and it's easier than crying, everyone looks beautiful when they're laughing, and it's a beautiful feeling when people make you laugh.

People reading this will obviously think I'm biased but let me tell you there's no one better to have a coffee with if you're feeling down. Mick makes me laugh every day and I know he'll make you laugh with his words. He'll make you laugh because we've all been there, we've all met at least one of the characters he brings to life. These are not just the experiences of the author they are the experiences of life and what we do when life throws these little trials in our way. By reading this book you are realising the final part of the writer's dream, writing is only the start of it, a storyteller needs an audience otherwise their trade is null and void, writers need to bring pleasure through their words and Mick is no exception. He is a storyteller who has always wanted to bring enjoyment to others, but only now, after thirty years, has he realised that he really can do what he has always wanted to do. The writer trapped in a businessman's body has broken free and this is his journey. It takes guts to stand at the top of a cliff looking down and then simply walk away, it takes even more guts to write so honestly about it. Once again I remember my bias, but I think he has attained so much more than zero, but why don't you read on and make up your own mind.

Thanks

       Hannah

INTODUCTION
by Michael J. Flynn

"Why did you choose to get married to your wife?" the therapist asked me.
"Because I loved her," I snapped back.
I didn't expect the head doctor to be so direct, I thought we were going to open with something gentle like, 'Were you breast fed as a child?' or 'Did your Father ever insert blunt instruments up your bottom?' No, I was a need case, and need dictated a direct route to the core of the problem.
"Why did you love her?" he continued.
I wanted to say 'Great tits' to lighten the atmosphere but I didn't think he'd appreciate it. The truth was I didn't know. I had met Karen when money and power had been my false Gods and I was different now.
"It was a long time ago," I said.
"Think about it then."

The book you are about to read is a snapshot of my heart so handle it carefully. Baring your soul so openly on paper is a frightening experience and after you read this you might like me or you might not, whatever your feelings I hope you appreciate the honesty of the work. Now before I start building myself up as some great storyteller, let me tell you I'm an ordinary man. Look at my photo on the back, I'm so average that dogs don't even bark at me, *but please*, do read on.

This is a story for anyone who's lost hope in themselves or the rest of the world. If I was a medical man I could describe it as the Beecham Powders for the heart, likewise if I was a car salesman I could describe it as the XR3I of personal journeys, but I'm neither of these things. This is the story of a man who split up with his wife, left his job, had a breakdown, went back to education and found himself. I know I'm not a rarity because these sort of things happen to a lot of people, but how many times do we celebrate the triumphs of an *average* man?

In 1997 I started evening classes to become a counsellor, not the wisest thing to do when you're having marital problems but I attended all the same. I'd got to that crossroads at twenty-seven where I'd wanted to do something different with my life, and further education seemed like a better option than dealing with soft drugs. Anyway, from the outside looking in it seemed like an easy qualification: an hours reading, class discussion and an eight hundred word journal every week. Shit, I could do that standing on my head, *and* manage to chuck in a few group hugs too. It was an interesting course, the people were really friendly just like you'd expect them to be, and the tutor was worldly wise in a way I'd never seen before. I loved it! The great thing about the course was that you could put whatever you wanted in your journal every week (as long as it related in some way to the syllabus). At first I figured I'd be witty because there's always humour in disaster, but as the course continued I became incredibly sad. You see, my life at home was dissolving fast, my hair was getting long and my wife was ever more distant, I didn't feel so funny anymore. After my marriage finished I gave up the course because I didn't have enough zest inside of me to do all the searching that was needed, but I did carry on with a journal entry every week. This time I did it differently though, instead of doing it for someone else I did it for me, and instead of looking at all the sad things in my life I started writing about all of the funny things. It was a really good idea because I figured if I got down I could just flick through a few pages and cheer myself up. Of course it didn't work, how could I ever expect something so simple to work, but it did seem to make other people smile, and the rest is publishing history. So put the kettle on, turn the pages, and help me exorcise a few demons. This is a true story.

ACKNOWLEDGEMENTS

*To my darling Hannah C. Beaumont, you gave me the gift of laughter and hope when I needed it most. Your drunken cartwheels are still the most impressive thing I've ever seen.

*To my Mother, Sylvia. I'm not gay I just fancied a career change.

*To my Father, Bernie. Your gift of stretching the truth truly motivates me.

*To Guy Gibson (St. Stock RC Maidstone). You were the only teacher to ever inspire me, thank you.

*To my Sister, Penny. Just thank you for putting up with me.

*To Mark Jenkins (University of Glamorgan). Out of all the drama lecturers I've met, you're the only one who doesn't steal the limelight away from the students.

*To Shirley Williams. Thank you.

*To Uncle Liam. Please forgive me.

*To Uncle Pat, Uncle Johnny and Uncle Mick. If they want another book it'll be about you three.

*And finally to Karen. I wish you luck, health and happiness, I know now I was never enough for you.

DEDICATION

I'd like to dedicate this book to two people who have changed my life and made it richer.

To Mike Schofield (My Mentor). God took you away before I ever had the chance to thank you. You were a true friend and I know you're thrashing all the angels and saints on the golf course in heaven.

To Hannah Beaumont. I promise to never propose to you on 'Trisha' but I will propose. Thank you, you've blessed the core of my life.

CHAPTER 1
Bright City Lights

Lying alone on claret soaked altar,
A naked city unvarnished in reverence.
Bright neon bringing forth religious devotion
To the rabid dogs who worship false gods.

I walked for miles on these streets laced with poison.
Looking for the shadow of your eyes in the lights.
I was bumped and shoved by the clan,
Who roam deliriously hoping to penetrate the blister of greed.
I took calm shelter in doorways,
Seeking answers to a host of unspeakable questions.
With all my indulgences exhausted,
I turned to the night and took my life.

For days I trudged round the streets trying to find my bearings, convincing myself that this was my *new life*, and that the sooner I started embracing it the happier I'd be. As I watched my marching feet on those wet pavements I tried to imagine the new tracks I would carve, and the way that everything was going to be different now. Stuff like this is supposed to be liberating, but freedom must have eluded me because I only ever felt sad at my predicament. Sorrowful for my guilt and bitter about my history.

All these doubts had started some six months earlier with what the doctor had described as, 'a manic episode brought on by marital stress'. I had really flipped out and scared everyone by loosing a couple of days immersed in panic attacks and paranoia, even now I'm still coming to terms with the fact that I'm not immortal. Being weak like this isn't a nice feeling, having a flawed suit of armour suddenly makes everything hurt more and I there I was stuck in the middle drowning, and nobody even noticed. So I left. I stood up, looked at the core of my life and didn't like what I could see, and left. It wasn't anything brave people fall out of love everyday, I'd just become wearied with my life and decided to change it all before I became bitter, and that was the biggest problem. In leaving my wife I couldn't decide whether I'd been selfish or compassionate. There wasn't anyone else involved if there had been things would have been easier to understand. This was all about us and the reality that we couldn't make each other happy anymore, if we could have just said this when things had started to go wrong, we would have saved ourselves both a lot of discomfort. Instead we locked horns and battled to the death, ripping up years of friendship with the kind of truths that two people should never utter to one another. Now I was here, lost and confused, with too many tears it seemed that my whole life had become an oxymoron that was cancelling itself out. I couldn't be Michael Flynn anymore that person was dead and buried but at the same time I didn't know who I was becoming. I longed for some make believe fairy with a magic wand to take it all away, but if someone had asked me what I needed to make myself happy I wouldn't have been able to tell them anyway. I was a right mess, I knew I desired independence but at the same time I also wanted to belong to something, I resented my wife but I also loved her at the same time.

So as I walked those streets I tried to rationalise my decisions by taking a step outside myself and looking in for the first time. As a person I was made up of so many different things, some of them I loved and some of them I hated but they were *all mine*, and they were *all me*. Every experience every emotion my life was made up of little short stories that brought me to this place, this place that I would now call home.

MY UNCLE LIAM

A piece of would-be advice to all partners planning to become couples: before getting serious with anyone, first meet all of their family members. Then and only then will you have a true understanding of what your partner is, and what they could have possibly become if history had been different.

My Father had four brothers: one was a successful liar, one was a gambling alcoholic, one was a would-be alcoholic who could never take the pace and Liam, the runt of the litter, was a 'musical' alcoholic for want of a better description. Love him or hate him Liam was a man without discrimination in his soul: Liam would drink anything, anything at all especially if it was free. His anti-discriminatory drinking habits caused him great loss over the years but he was never prepared to give up alcohol, maybe because it was the only constant in his life. He didn't have a partner, that ship had long since sailed when he found his first true love in bed with another man, and he no longer had full-time employment. Drunks can't hold jobs down. All this paints an extremely poor picture of Liam and that's not fair, because although flawed in many ways Liam still had a huge heart. It was this same huge heart combined with the same alcohol consumption that sometimes made life a little challenging for him.

Liam had two good drinking friends who lived above a pub called the Anglesey Arms in Woolwich High Street. Maggie and Tom. Maggie was a sixties throwback with beads and bangles *still* in her hair. Her love of peace and Jimi Hendrix was only surpassed by her love of Jack Daniel's and soft drugs. She was a drunk. Tom on the other hand was a charming bounder with a wonderful knowledge of British literature.

Unfortunately his charm would transmogrify into something quite ugly under the influence of booze. He too was a drunk. Maggie and Tom had been to hell and back at least a dozen times, and on the last return trip had brought a dog back with them called Daisy. Unable to have children themselves they took to the roles of parenthood and made the mutt from 'destination unknown' their baby. Of course Daisy wasn't flustered by this, she lapped it up, all twelve stones of it to be precise. This was the only dog in south-east London to have a high cholesterol problem, but none of that mattered because as a family unit they could cope with anything. So when Liam found Maggie, Tom, and Daisy in the Anglesey Arms looking miserable he was confused. People who had holidays planned to commence at the weekend were usually full of excitement and glee. He hadn't had a holiday himself but he had seen others, you could spot them a mile off: arms filled with travel brochures boring friends and family with stories about bikini's and suntan lotions, you know what I'm talking about. Yet here today sat his two holiday going chums with faces like wet weekends and not a holiday brochure in sight. What was going on? Liam crept over.

'Evening, the usual I suppose? A pint, a J.D. and a packet of pork scratchings for Daisy.'

Tom lifted his sorrowful head.

'Oh hello Liam, No we're alright, we're just having a quiet night.'

'Don't want to be hung over on the plane, *very wise* if you ask me.'

Then something strange happened, Maggie's eyes filled with tears, and Tom gulped as if he knew what was coming, Liam suspected a can of worms had been opened.

'We're not going!'

Liam stood still for a second unsure of how to continue, knowing he had come into a conversation part way through was a vexatious position to be in.

'What do you mean you're not going?'

Maggie burst into tears and ran to the ladies toilet for sanctuary, Liam could hear her wails from the public bar.

'What the hell's going on Tom?'

'The kennels doubled booked us, they only let us know a couple of hours ago and we fly at one.'

Liam looked confused.

'Well book Daisy into another kennels, they can't all be full.'

Tom sighed it was obviously something he had already suggested to the blubbering Maggie.

'If only it was that simple.'

Liam knew he was digging himself a hole but the drama was so intriguing that he just had to ask.

'Well what's confusing about that?'

'It's Daisy, she knows one of the assistants at that particular kennels. She used to clip her toes at the local vets and was always very gentle with her.'

'Yeah, so?'

'Well Maggie won't let daisy lodge with strangers, she thinks it'll upset her.'

Liam laughed.

'She a fucking dog Tom, not heir to the bloody throne. Stick the damn mutt in another kennels, and buy her some chocolate when you come home.'

'Don't you think I'd do that if I could? *It's not me*, it's her. That dog is *her* bloody baby'

Maggie let a large moan go from the toilets. Point taken, Liam thought.

'How long is that going to last Tom?'

Liam said, referring to the moaning

'Two weeks she said, the same duration as the holiday we were supposed to go on.'

Liam tried not to laugh as he stared at the mangy dog that had caused so much trouble.

'Are you sure you won't have that drink? I'm going to the bar anyway. Daisy looks like she could murder a packet of pork scratchings.'

'Okay, get one for Maggie too, it might calm her nerves.'

Liam trudged to the bar troubled by his friend's sad demeanour, he ordered the drinks and scratchings and then thought of solutions for his friends. He knew it wasn't really his problem but he hated seeing people upset. Besides, Maggie and Tom were old friends of his and being the good Samaritan he saw it as his responsibility to help. Liam placed the drinks and snacks on a tray, and made his way back to Tom and Maggie who had now returned from the ladies powder room. Never good with upset people he handed the drinks out in silence, but this time Tom had a whopping great smile on his face.

'Thanks Liam, you're a great friend, did I ever tell you that?'

Liam wondered if it was something in the beer because Tom was only nice to the opposite sex, unless he had grown a pair of breasts or something.

'Thanks Tom.'

Tom chipped in again.

'Tell me, you come from a big close family, did you ever have pets as you were growing up?'

'Of course we did, my Brother managed a pet shop. We had cats, rabbits, budgies and dogs, we always had loads of dogs.'

Tom's smile widened.

'So you like animals then?'

'Of course I like animals, the only reason I don't have a dog now is that it wouldn't fit in with my cosmopolitan life style.'

As soon as Liam had answered that question he knew he was being set up for something, Tom's rapid mood change followed by his 'nice-ness' just didn't add up. Never a man to be played Liam decided to take charge and ask the question that he knew was on Tom's lips.

'Look, I know Daisy and Daisy knows me, I'm probably the closest thing she has to an Uncle. Why don't I look after Daisy while you're away?'

Maggie's disposition brightened immediately.

'Oh Liam we couldn't put on you like that, what would people say?'

'Well the offer's there Maggie.'

Tom nearly dived across the table, he wasn't about to get this close to the Costa Del Sol and have Maggie blow it away with good manners. This holiday was an opportunity for him to catch some well-earned 'rays' and enjoy the odd San Miguel or two, Lord knows he needed a break from being on the wagon .

'Of course it would help us greatly, and we'd give you thirty quid for dog food'.

'Thirty quid, what does she eat, steak!'

Maggie interrupted, eager to justify the alleged overspend.

'Daisy needs her vitamins, otherwise her coat will lose its shine.'

Daisy needs a good kick up the ass and some more exercise Liam thought, he didn't spend that much on food for himself.

'Well Maggie, rest assured I'll make sure she continues to get them, when you come back her coat will shine with all the rich colours of a Spanish sunset.'

That's all she wanted to hear.

Just before closing time Maggie and Tom departed for warmer climates leaving Daisy in the safe care of an extremely happy Liam. He had come out of the evening smelling of roses, not only had he gained a faithful friend for the next two weeks, he now had an extra thirty pounds tucked away neatly in his back pocket. How's that for a result?

Although she wasn't human Daisy kind of knew that her pet food budget in Liam's charge was never going to be spent on Pedigree Chum. Giving an alcoholic the choice between John Smith's and her dietary requirements meant a very hungry fortnight.

'So Daisy what should we do with the rest of the evening? Come on, anything you like, I'm flush with money at the moment.'

Daisy looked on in an uninterested manner why did she always get stuck with the drunks at the end of the evening who wanted to engage her in human conversation that she didn't understand?

Liam belched, he was extremely comfortable. Maggie and Tom had bought him drinks all night as way of a small thank-you for his help, but now he was hungry. This was not out of the ordinary because he would often be ravenous for food especially when he'd been on a three or four day bender where he'd just simply forgotten to eat. He finished his last gulp of beer.

'What do you say to a chicken madras Daisy, you must be fed up of that dog food they're feeding you? How about spicing up your life a little'

It was a good point, I mean, if someone served me up the same cold mush everyday with a handful of smelly biscuits I'd savour a chicken madras too, regardless of the consequences. This didn't seem madness to Liam, the way he saw it was that both foods gave you 'death breath' and both foods probably had the same ingredients, so what was the problem? Chicken madras it was, chicken madras with a Nan bread, chicken madras, a Nan bread and a bottle of vodka from the off license next door. Sorted. Liam purchased the vodka first he was a man of priorities. Thirty pounds didn't go far these days and if it was a choice between an extra Nan bread or some moonshine, the moonshine always won.

Daisy was a willing accomplice though because the off license had a stand full of pork scratchings but when they got to the takeaway daisy waited outside. She wasn't stupid, she had seen other dogs enter these establishments and never be seen again, besides the name 'Daisy Dansak' didn't have the right feel to it. As she sat patiently Liam entered the establishment, money exchanged hands, and then with arms heavily laden they made their way home with Daisy walking dutifully behind, off of the lead. Safety was a concern but a man with two arms full of warm grease doesn't have the luxury of carrying a dogs leash too.

Inside his flat Liam couldn't wait to plunder his booty, not the curry, but the vodka of course, the curry was placed by the sofa to cool down. He wasn't interested in the logistics of restaurant ownership, but so many takeaway cartons for fifteen pounds, how *did* they manage to make a profit? First there was the cost of the ingredients, rice, chicken, and onions, he sighed, they weren't cheap these days *even* when they were on special offer at Tesco's. Then there was the spices, mustn't forget the spices because they *must* cost at least a pound a jar. It was all adding up far too quickly. Finally he estimated the wage cost for the whole operation, and working on minimum wage projections the lowest cost he could get to was sixteen pounds and seventy-five pence. Damn! He hated taking advantage of people like this, maybe someone should give these guys a lesson in money management? Thinking of all his Indian friends working in the sweaty takeaway kitchens across the country was a thirsty thought. So, while the curry was cooling the vodka was casually poured. Vodka was great for killing time.

Liam looked through the smeared window at Russia's crystal beauty, and ran a large gulg through his teeth stinging his gums. Vodka was tough love, but according to Oprah Winfrey weren't all relationships? He took another gulg, Daisy whined and looked down at the curry, she was hungry.

'Okay, just let your Uncle Liam have a little drink then he'll fetch you the biggest feed this side of South East London.'

Liam went to take another sip but his glass was empty so he poured a second glass of Moscow's malt and patted the dog who was still waiting for the sodding curry to cool down. Although his night had been euphoric his happiness was now distracted by Daisy's hunger. Why did those underpaid Indians have to make their damn food so hot? It wasn't that difficult, he himself had read the vesta instructions on many occasions and had never crucified a boil-in-the bag curry to this day.

'Don't worry Daisy, another five minutes and we'll be in Bombay heaven.'

Another drink, another five minutes, that damn curry was *still* too hot. Maybe he should just lie on the sofa here for five minutes, maybe he should just close his eyes while the food reaches its correct temperature. Yes, that would be a good idea. Liam fell asleep.

It was eight a.m. the door of his flat was caught by a draught and slammed shut. Liam's eyes opened slightly. Shit! He had forgotten to close the front door again, why did he do that whenever he had a drink? Why was he in such a hurry to get home all the time? Soon he'd do that once too often and someone would pinch all of his stuff while he was asleep, and then what would he do? Nobody had time for a drunken fools woes in Woolwich, why should they the borough was full of them. He closed his eyes again and decided not to worry about it, he didn't need to get up right now, Daisy wouldn't need a walk for a couple of hours. Shit! Daisy! Liam sat bolt upright on the sofa, poor Daisy would be gnarling her bloody paws by now. So, with eyes still half-shut and unable to focus Liam called her.

'Daisy, Daisy come here girl, I haven't forgotten you I'm sure the food's cool enough to eat now.'

Silence rang from all the rooms in the little flat and Liam felt wicked.

'Come on Daisy, I haven't forgotten you honest I haven't.'

In the silence Liam's vision returned. Where the hell was she? He looked down at the piece of carpet where the takeaway cartons had sat and could see that Daisy had taken matters into her own hands, she had opened every single carton in the yellow carrier bag and eaten its contents. Nothing was spared, not even the onions and mint sauce for the popadoms, she had eaten the lot! Now he *was* worried.

'Daisy, come on girl, I know your stomach's hurting but it's no good hiding. I can't help you if you hide.'

Liam got up from his slumber and tried to remember where he put the Andrews liver salts but had to hold his head because those vodka headaches always held on. He turned three hundred and sixty degrees perusing all four corners of the studio but still couldn't see the elusive Daisy. Where was she? And then he noticed the green carpet, or what was left of its green pattern now that it was covered in loose dog excrement. There was crap everywhere, piles of it in the living room and puddles of it in the kitchen. Some of it in noticeable chunk shapes and some of it resembling modern art in the hallway as it splashed neatly up the skirting boards. It was on everything and it stank like hell!

Daisy's marked absence initially had Liam thinking that she had simply shit herself to death in a curry like stupor, but after he failed to locate her carcass in the flat he had to consider other conclusions. Maybe she'd taken herself for a walk, maybe she was ashamed of her bowel movements and run off, maybe she gone back to the takeaway for a second helping of friendly Asian bacteria. Either way he had to find her because Daisy was something much more than a dog to both Maggie and Tom, but what should he do?

I mean, did the Police having a 'missing dogs' facility or was it down to him to check out all the local K9 haunts? He took a deep breath to calm himself down nothing was going to be achieved if he remained in this mood. So after a cigarette and vodka chaser Liam decided that the best thing to do was to go out and look for her, for all he knew she could be sitting outside in the front garden sunning herself. He brushed his teeth, put his walking shoes on and left the little flat on his own. First he tried the common, then he tried the little park down by the ferry because he knew these were her favourite walks, but still she was nowhere to be seen. Unperturbed by his failures he tried Woolwich High Street, and then in a state of near panic walked all the way up to Shooters Hill to check if she'd wandered up that way. Nothing!

Liam didn't fancy the long haul back from Shooters Hill so he caught the number seventy-three bus back from the Police station on the corner. He begrudged paying the pound bus fare calculating it to be about the same price as half a lager, but if he walked he would surely miss the first hour of opening time, and he *never* missed his lunchtime drink for anyone. Apart from the continual starting and stopping being on the bus was good because it gave him some thinking time, the kind of time he needed to clear his head and reflect on his options. There was Maggie and Tom, friends of his who had entrusted their surrogate baby into his care. There was the thirty pound food budget that had now been spent on curry and booze, and there was the medical concern of Daisy's bowels not to mention her absence. Things were not looking rosy for Liam, in twenty-four hours he had spent the money and rotted Daisy's intestines whilst in the process of loosing her from his custody, not the kind of mistakes Mary Poppins would have made he thought. It wasn't really his fault though, I mean, what kind of parents would leave their child in the charge of an alcoholic anyway?

The bell rang for Liam's stop, he thought he'd have a quick drink and then report the dog as a missing person at Woolwich Police station. He knew it wouldn't be on crime watch or anything, but if the worst came to the worst and Daisy wasn't found, he'd like to show Maggie and Tom that he'd covered all angles by reporting it to the correct authorities. Off the bus he staggered with his nine o'clock shadow and in to the closet pub he walked, as I mentioned, Liam was never a man of discrimination, he would drink anywhere.

'A pint of Mild for the slow lane, and vodka for the fast lane.'

'Coming right up poppet.'

A chirpy barman said with a wink, Liam smiled nervously back. There was a time not so long ago when a casual wink between men implied something quite complicated, now everyone was doing it even the staff at the Lord Raglan. (A Pub) Liam mimicked the barman's voice.

' *'Coming right up poppet'*. I'd shove that vodka up your ass if I didn't think you'd get pleasure from it.' What kind of man calls another man 'poppet' in broad daylight? Anyone would think he was gay. The little barman skipped back with the drinks.

'How much?'

Liam barked in his most masculine voice. This would surely dampen any winking, blinking or air kissing.

'No, no, these are on me. I always buy the first drink for a new face.'

He winked again and skipped off to serve a huge guy at the end of the bar who was wearing what looked like a leather hat with chains. What the hell was going on? Liam was confused, but not as confused as Bonny Langford behind the bar. He couldn't sit here all day and let a man he'd never met before buy him drinks, it didn't make sense. His Father had a name for people like that! But, after gazing at the amber and crystal colours sitting on the bar Liam had a change of heart, well maybe he wasn't supposed to understand everything in this life.

What was so wrong about one man doing another man a good turn by buying him a drink? It didn't mean he was gay or anything, it was just an unselfish act constructed to create a good karma. In fact that was it, the barman wasn't gay, he was a Buddhist, a Buddhist monk from East Woolwich doubling as a barman so he could spread some good karma around. Liam relaxed and drunk his drinks. The bar wasn't so bad, alright the music was a bit loud but he liked the feel of it. They'd obviously spent a lot of money on the interior, not the kind he'd have at his home, but he loved the blue carpet with its little pink triangles in the middle. The bar was well stocked too all manner of weird and wonderful spirits sat on the shelves, blue stuff from Jamaica, red stuff from China and brown stuff from Bulgaria. All the bottles were arranged vertically underneath a patch of wall called the 'Pink Hall of Fame.' On this wall were signed photographs of musicians he'd never heard of: The Pet Shop Boys, Jimmy Somerville, Marc Almond, etc. Strange that they should dedicate a wall to a group of small time musicians though, why wasn't Elvis or Jerry Lee up there? I mean, I bet Elvis alone had achieved more number ones than all the Somerville's and Almond's put together. How come they rated so high in this bar? It didn't make sense.

'Same again?'

Startled by the voice Liam looked down, remarkably his drinks were finished. When would public houses realise that the only way forward was larger measures, that way customers wouldn't always be prematurely finishing their drinks.

'Oh, yes please, but only half a lager this time.'

The barman smiled a toothy grin.

'Coming right up, and by the way, has anyone told you you've got beautiful eyes?'

That was it! That was as much as he could stand, if the barman wasn't buying *this* round he'd tell the bastard to stick the drinks where the sun didn't shine and leave the pub with his integrity still intact. Having a man winking and buying drinks was one thing but complimenting him on the beauty of his eyes was a completely different kettle of fish. In Liam's Victorian world there was an invisible line between courtesy and fetish and he'd just crossed it with both feet.

'That'll be three pound twenty please.'

Liam painted an indignant look across his face, he wanted the whole pub including the butch man with the hat to know he wasn't a fruitcake.

'I don't know what manner of *gay* establishment this is, but I will *not* be having those drinks. I've decided to take my business elsewhere. Besides, I've got a dog to find.'

The barman looked hurt.

'Well if that's how you heterosexuals refer to your partners these days than I'm happy to be clean out of it, you're barred! Now get out before I call Samson the doorman.'

A doorman to remove him from the premises! He had never been so insulted in his whole life. In his forty plus years of drinking he had never been removed from anywhere. 'Samson the doorman'! He didn't need security to move him on he was leaving anyway, and not because Cindy Crawford behind the bar broke a poxy nail and decided to take it out on him either.

'Come on, *out*!'

'Don't worry I'm going'

Nothing could keep him there a second longer, he had a missing persons report to lodge at Woolwich Police Station and no number of free drinks would stand in his way. He had said his piece and now he was going.

Two hours later a dejected Liam with cigarette in mouth sat on the steps of Woolwich Police Station wondering what had gone wrong. Basically the Police had told him to piss off explaining that 'missing person's' posters were exclusively reserved for humans alone. This was unhelpful enough but when he asked them to keep an eye out for Daisy on the beat he was rudely told that their resources were far too thinly spread to allocate any man-hours to UFO sightings, crop circles or dog hunts. This really angered him, and if Liam had paid taxes he would have told them right there and then to keep a civil tongue in their heads because *he paid their bloody wages*. Being unemployed prevented him from delivering this line, but at least he thought it, a thought was almost as strong as a deed in his mind. Then it came to him, if the Police wouldn't help with a missing person's poster then he'd make one himself. That would show them wouldn't it? And when Daisy was found he'd take the little poster and place it right on the Desk Sergeant's counter. Right under his nose where he couldn't ignore it, and tell him, yes he'd tell him alright. 'All coppers are wankers'! Liam finished his cigarette and wandered home determined to change the course of his fate, the public services may have turned their backs on him but he was by no means a beaten man.

At home Liam quickly found some marker pens and an old piece of A4. Then he hit a stumbling block. He couldn't quite remember what Daisy looked like. She was 'yellowish' of course, he knew that much, but he couldn't quite remember her size or what her face looked like. After much internal debate the self-build missing person's poster read.

>Lost
>One yellow dog. (Colouring to be confirmed on sight)
>Average size and height.
>Pretty face.
>Answers to the name of Daisy.
>Five pounds reward!
>N.B *Dog may smell of curry.*

Five pounds was of course five pounds but he was desperate and he thought the lure of money would have every kid this side of the water looking for the mangy mutt. So he took the poster straight down to the convenience shop, paid his fifty pence and prayed. Liam was now happy that he had covered all of the angles. Placing an advert in the sweet shop window was the cheapest and most effective form of advertising in Woolwich, a system that his Mother and Father had sworn by.

After all of his efforts Liam felt like a drink, no amount of time sitting by the telephone would bring Daisy back any quicker. He daren't go into the Anglesey Arms though, in fear that the landlord may ask him how Daisy's was getting along. Sod it! He'd walk up the other end of town and have a swift one in the Rope Makers Arms. It was safe in there, no pink triangles or over-friendly barman, just a miserable landlord with a red nose and halitosis. Besides, it would be a good opportunity to put the word about. You know, see if anyone had seen a medium sized 'yellowish' dog smelling of curry, Lord knows what else he could do, except light a candle perhaps. So, making the sign of the cross Liam entered the Rope Makers Arms with the intention of expanding the perimeters of his search and having a drink. His hopes of discovering a lead were quickly dashed as he found the reception to his plight somewhat apathetic. The only lead coming from the red nosed landlord who informed Liam that *he* himself had a 'yellowish' dog upstairs who'd be down later to serve drinks behind the bar. Sarcasm was just one of the many services they offered at the Rope Makers Arms.

The following morning the telephone rang, Liam hoisted himself carefully off of the floor because those vodka headaches really hung on. He squinted, adjusting his eyes to the morning sun peeping its head through the open curtains. Right, now where did he put the telephone? He knew it was in the lounge somewhere because it sounded close, real close, but by the time he found it in the bread bin the caller had rung off. Frustration or old age, who knows? Anyway, having the new '1471' facility gave Liam the luxury of re-connecting with the last caller who thankfully turned out to be Billy Patel, the same convenience shop owner with the missing persons poster in his window. It appeared that Liam's prayers had been answered as Billy told him that there was a little tinker boy in the shop with a 'yellowish' dog matching Daisy's smell and description. Billy was as helpful as he could be, explaining that he could not have the dog on his premises for more than ten minutes in fear that the environmental health office would close him down again.

'Keep him there, I'll be down in five minutes I promise.'

Liam snapped down the receiver and put the phone back in the bread bin, this was perfect! He could now drink in the Anglesey Arms again. He'd have to celebrate of course, but all in good time. First he had a date with Billy Patel and tinker boy who found his dog.

'I got yar wee dog here.'

Liam looked at the sorry sight that had now become Daisy, she had certainly lost weight in the last twenty-four hours, and this was something he'd have to resolve before Maggie and Tom returned.

'Where did you find her?'

The tinker boy looked confused he hadn't come here to answer questions like that.

'Where?'

'Yeah, where did you find her?'

'Oh, nowhere special. Just up the road there, running round on her own like.'

Liam stroked Daisy's head and then questioned the little tinker boy some more. He figured that if he was to part with a 'fiver' he'd at least get his monies worth.

'Have you looked after her while you've had her?'

'What?'

Liam repeated the question asserting his authority, he had the money he had the power, and he wanted some answers to his questions,

'Have you looked after her while you've had her?'

But the little tinker boy was having none of it, his rationale registered that he had delivered the dog, and now wanted his money.

'Look fella, I'm sorry d'aliens forgot to remove your anal probe, but ye got ye dog, can I have my money now?'

Much as he hated to admit it Liam thought the boy had a point. He had after all brought a dog that complied to all the criteria on the missing person's poster, and now wanted payment in receipt of completion. What was unfair about that? Nothing! So Liam paid the boy and let him go on his way. So satisfied with the service he would have happily paid ten times the amount to be where he was now, man and dog re-united, and better still his friends would never find out.

'I guess my work is done Daisy. What do you say to a celebratory drink at the Anglesey?'

It was so nice for Liam to be able to go back into his local he was fed up of pink triangles and red noses, he wanted to see some over flowing ash trays and puddles of beer again, the 'Anglesey' was tailor made for these needs. If the truth be known it would probably help Daisy too by re-integrating her back into her social environment. That way she wouldn't suffer with post traumatic stress disorder at a later stage or something. Liam stroked Daisy, Maggie and Tom would be so proud of him for looking after her that way.

'Daisy, I'm not into spoiling dogs, but in light of your return why don't me and you bury the hatchet. Come on, I'll buy you a pint of scratchings.'

Daisy wagged her tail, she hadn't understood a single word of his babble but she liked the tone of Liam's voice so into the pub she followed.

'A pint of mild for me and half a dozen packets of scratchings for Daisy.'

Liam said to the barmaid.

'I wondered when you'd turn up.'

'What kind of welcome is that?'

The barmaid pulled the pint of mild from the pump and threw the packets of scratchings at Liam.

'Four pound twelve pence.'

What was up with her? Liam wasn't used to this kind of hostility, he was a man of peace

'Bad day?'

'I should shove that pint of mild right up your ass.'

Now he was worried. Twenty-four hours away from the Anglesey Arms and *suddenly* the whole world hated him. He thought the best way to handle it was to walk away, she'd probably calm down later and apologise with a drink on the house or something. Liam turned to walk away.

'Who are the *damn* scratchings for?'

Liam was no longer worried, he was now frightened. Firstly she had asked an obvious question to which there was *only* an obvious answer, and secondly she had shown anger by using the word *'damn'*. This could only mean one of two things, either he had inadvertently pissed her off, or Daisy had.

'The scratchings?'

'Yes Liam, the *scratchings*.'

'Why they're for Daisy of course.'

The barmaid blew a gasket.

'Well you better take them upstairs to her then!'

'Why would I want to do that? She's standing here with me.'

Liam didn't know what to do, everything he said seemed to add fuel to the fire.

'I don't know who you bought that *fucking* dog off, but that *is not Daisy*. Daisy's upstairs. She turned up here last night after you lost her. And it'll take a lot more good will than six packets of poxy scratchings to get the shit out of my living room carpet you drunken wanker.'

Stress is when you wake up screaming and realise you haven't been to sleep yet. Liam *was* a drunken wanker, he had lost a dog and re-found the wrong one. This wasn't a celebration, it was a nightmare: five pound down, a flat covered in shit and a barmaid who hated him, not to mention a dog that he now had to get rid of. Maybe he could bluff it.

'What do you mean Daisy's upstairs? She's standing right here don't you recognise her?'

The barmaid leant over the bar so she was nose to nose with Liam.

'Listen, as you may have gathered I am not a fucking people person. I work forty hours a week to be this poor. I empty ashtrays, I pull pints and I clean toilets. *I am not, I repeat 'not' paid to pick dog shit out of carpets though.* And before you try to convince me that's bloody Daisy make sure you get the colour right.'

'What do you mean?'

Liam questioned, as the barmaid spat from between her teeth.

'Daisy's a fucking black Labrador you twat!'

Great! Even his lies were flawed. What was he going to do now? Liam wanted to ask her if she was *sure,* but he knew he could end up with a personal injury so he just drank his drink and left with his new pet, lovingly renamed 'Biddy'. Much as he loved dogs he knew he couldn't keep Biddy his journey was for one, anyone else would just be a back seat driver who held him up. Liam's only consolation was the fact that logically you couldn't loose a lost dog. Meaning, that if he was to set Biddy free on Woolwich common he wouldn't be breaking any laws or absconding his duties as a surrogate Father. Please don't make judgements of my biased story though, because I do think I'm painting a bad picture of Liam again. I mean, he wasn't totally without feeling, he'd make sure she was alright and everything. Of course he would, he'd open the six packs of scratchings and leave them with her, that way she wouldn't starve or anything, he was a real Francis of Assisi.

Up to Woolwich Common he walked, taking another bus would have ate further into his drinking money and he didn't want that. Biddy walked close to him on the bit of rope that the little tinker boy supplied, as sure as eggs were eggs she could feel abandonment coming. Somehow she knew all the RSPCA posters in the world wouldn't save her from a night under the stars now. The best she could look forward to was a future standing outside Woolworth's selling the 'Big Issue' with some scraggy nomad who hadn't bathed in a year.

Liam whistled 'MacNamara's Band' under his breath. The last twenty-fours hours of his life had been not only the most tiring, but also the most stressful. He crossed the road onto the common and smiled, because in about five minutes he would be a free man again with no responsibilities, no debts and no injuries. Things were finally coming to a close, he'd let Biddy off to make her own way in life with a feed of scratchings in her belly, and then return to the Anglesey Arms to make his peace with the barmaid. Surely Daisy couldn't have made as much mess at the pub as she had in his flat. I mean, how much curry can a three-foot dog squeeze out of its anus in twenty-four hours?

'Oi you.'

Liam saw a burly looking man running towards him from across the common.

'I want a word with you.'

Strange, Liam didn't recognise him, but then maybe he was mistaking him for someone else or something. It happened all the time, more often than not shop owners mistook him for a Saturday night drunk who urinated in their doorways and windows, strange that.

As the man grew closer Liam could see he was troubled. It was the foaming mouth that sort of gave it away, but how was he to know that this anger was directed at him? He opened his mouth to greet the stranger right as the bothered man swung his fist to hit his head. Pain and confusion clouded Liam's mind as a succession of quick blows struck his torso with incredible accuracy. What the hell was going on? Why would someone want to attack him like this? The man stood back pleased with his work and spat on Liam's crumpled body. Liam was waiting for Biddy to jump in at any second and save him the same way 'Lassie' would have in the films. He even let out a little groan to entice her into growling or something, but nothing. Not once, not once through the whole fifteen second confrontation had Biddy stood up for him! She just sat there and wagged her tail as if she knew the bloody guy.

'You know what's worse than thieves like you?'

Liam was now on his feet but scared to ask.

'I'll tell you what's worse than thieves like you. It's thieves like you that get kids to do their dirty work for them.'

Liam held his side trying to squeeze a sentence out in between stomach cramps it proved more difficult than he thought.

'What are you talking about?'

The kind stranger leapt forward and slapped his face with an open hand, this question had seemed to anger him again.

'Fancy getting a child to steal a dog just so you could get a lousy five pound reward. I've been up all night with my *crying kids* because of you.'

For about the hundredth time that day Liam was in the wrong place at the wrong time.

'You've got me mixed up with someone else, *what dog, and what kid are you talking about*?'

The kind man pulled a face indicating confusion, he finally clicked that Liam had no idea what he was talking about. This bafflement set all kinds of balls into play: Liam was considering 'plight' and 'fright' whilst his assailant was still all hung up over 'fight'. A second's silence passed between them as the man tried to figure out if Liam was lying or not.

'Why, that dog down there.'

He said pointing at Biddy. Liam was beginning to click.

'And the kid?'

Liam questioned.

'The little tinker boy you got to steal her from my garden. When I caught him climbing over my fence again he told me the whole story.'

Liam shrugged his shoulders, there was probably no point explaining the whole thing to this man, he wouldn't believe him anyway, besides he needed a drink now to calm his nerves. There were too many freaks in this world and not enough circuses, and this thought was enough to turn someone to drink.

CHAPTER 2
This Ain't It

No consequences of rueful energy in this biosphere,
Never considering for isolation as before.
There's hundreds and thousands of them,
Malleable individuals immersed in one another.
For the first time loaded with blueberry puff-cheeks,
Belly laughing with wintry contentment.
Oh the innocent warmth of sharing,
The innocent fairytale that makes me feel guilty.
I never meant to come with baggage,
But now my arms are full.

I moved into this little pad right outside the university with three female pupils, thinking that if I was to return to full-time education I should at least be around other learned students for inspiration. New lodgings was a frightening step because it meant there really was no turning back, and when I unpacked my bags and turned the lights out on the first night I knew I had no one else to impress except myself from now on. I cried myself to sleep for the first four days.

The house was a snug little place with built in wardrobes and bags of room, the kind of abode that estate agents would say had potential, and I was happy in this property. Apart from the lumpy bed my room was perfect, I had finally done what millions of other people had wanted to do. I had escaped, I had escaped the rat race by simply opting out of it and here I was embarking on a new journey, twenty-nine, single and free, nothing holding me back except the missing mattress slats on my bed.

I wish the same could have been said for the poor old bathroom though, living with three females placed certain infringements on my personal hygiene. I'm not one to bitch but let's just say that there were silent rules regarding my usage of the WC Silent rules that dictated a time slot of five minutes between 8.15 and 8.20 am. This was not a favourable environment for a dawn grouch who likes to take his time in the mornings, even worse when you've got a hangover. On these mornings I would be antagonistic and take my time, sometimes up to twenty minutes just for the hell of it. This kind of pettiness led to animosity and in time, arguments. Being a man who didn't like to be around anger I took to drinking to avoid any further confrontations with the three women who had become my surrogate family.

My First Love

She didn't like me, and that's what was alluring I think. If I'd been younger I would have pulled her pigtails, but as a fifteen-year old boy I saw it as some kind of challenge. You see, teenage boys hate to be told, 'no' or 'go away weirdo' because when a teenager's hormones are raging a woman saying, 'no' represents nothing more than foreplay. Carla had not only said 'no' to me, she had completely ignored me for a period of six weeks and the whole thing was driving me crazy. Conventional means had failed by this time, so I started watching her, following her movements hoping we could bump into one another by chance. This was okay for a bit but my patience gave way after a while, I *desperately* wanted to talk to her. Not all was lost though, she was a creature of habit and I now knew her routine, so I did the one thing I promised I'd never do, and joined the church youth club as a fully paid member. Normally I wouldn't attend something like this because these venues were traditionally reserved for the more conservative members of the school, but then Carla was no ordinary woman either.

My insincere entrance caused a bit of a stir amongst the bible bashers who felt I was trespassing on their turf. They felt I didn't belong to their little gathering because I was usually the person who ruined RE lessons for them by sitting at the back of the class pelting them with spit-balls. As it happened the task of wangling a conversation with Carla was easier than I'd anticipated, that night the numbers were odd so I was paired off with her for prayers. She had a tough exterior for people like me, but after I made her laugh we were both able to drop our guards long enough to enjoy each others company.

We had only spoken for about ten minutes, but in my world of cheap green aftershave and Duran Duran records 'no' secretly meant 'yes', and 'yes' meant begging her telephone number out of a friend.

I was *so* nervous the first time I called her that I took the precaution of writing out a little script, you know, to return to if I found myself running out of words. The last thing I wanted was to dry up and revert to old Monty Python scripts for cheap laughs. I tapped her number into the phone with a pair of extremely shaky hands and thought about her, Carla Dagostini, it was only a name but the two words placed together elicited the strongest of responses. The phone rang four times before she answered, I cleared my throat and put on my best telephone voice.

'Hello, can I speak to Carla.'
'Speaking'

Great, what do I say now I thought. I looked at my script for assistance but for some reason I couldn't read the words.

'Who am I speaking to?'

She inquired.

'Mick.'

'Mick who?'

This put my back up immediately, had our Earth shattering ten-minute conversation been forgotten already?

'Mick Flynn, you know, the guy from the youth club.'

'Oh, *that* Mick, what can I do for you?'

My heart sank, I didn't expect a tickertape reception but I had hoped that she'd at least be excited to hear from me. I stuttered, afraid that I had cocked everything up by misjudging her enthusiasm for me.

'Well, I was wondering, you know, if you're not too busy, if you'd like to go to a Valentines disco on Thursday.'

'Who with?'

She laughed. This was a woman who understood playing hard to get inside out.

'Me of course.'

Silence travelled back up the phone line, and I wondered whether she had cut me off in fits of mirth or disgust, I mean, as a mere mortal at the gates of heaven I was hardly worthy.

'Are you asking me out on a date?'

I hesitated, unsure of how to continue.

'Yes, I think I am.'

Silence sounded for the second time, and I prayed that she'd let me down gently by telling me she was washing her hair or something. To crush me acidulously at this stage would have left my heart shattered in a million pieces and I'd only just repaired it from the last six-week brush off.

'Okay, but just as friends because I don't know you that well.'

I couldn't believe my ears, 'okay' was as close to 'yes' as you could get. 'Okay' meant that we could hold hands at the end of the evening and people who walked home hand in hand *always* ended up as couples. I was so happy I wanted to kneel down and thank God for creating word 'Carla'. Thank him for creating the phone, and thank him for ordaining Saint Valentine.

'What time shall I pick you up?'

'Is seven o'clock okay?'

Of course seven o'clock was okay, one a.m. would have been okay, anytime would have been okay just as long as we both went to the dance together.

'Seven's fine, shall I bring anything?'

'Like what?'

'I don't know, a bottle of wine for your parents or something.'

This really tickled her for some reason and for the third time during our conversation I was on the other end of her laughter.

'No, no, leave the wine at home my parents are distrusting enough.'

I knew what she meant, for I too had a suspicious Mother who took instant dislike to strangers bearing gifts. '*Kindness at a cost*' she would say, and on some level I could relate to this, you know, *'beware of the naked man offering you his shirt'*. Pity that the Virgin Mary didn't consider this when the three wise men turned up though, because look what happened to him.

'Alright I'll leave the wine at home.'

'Great.'

We were really cooking now.

'I guess I'll see you on Thursday at seven then.'

'I'll look forward to it. Oh, and Mick. Be on time, there's nothing more I hate than people being late.'

I thought it was best to reassure her.

'Don't worry about that I'm always early, sometimes by *at least* half an hour.'

I'm sure I could hear her smile on the other end of the telephone and this made me happy.

'I've got to go now, I've got some homework to do, I'll see you on Thursday at seven okay.'

The phone went down and I ran round the room performing a victory dance for the dog who was the only person present in the house at the time. It's not the usual type of behaviour I'd prescribe too, but these circumstances were nothing short of exceptional.

The following day I took a peek inside my wardrobe and decided that it was time for a new outfit, because much as I liked batwing shirts and stay-press trousers they were hardly cutting edge. I needed something that was going to ooze class, something urban and mysterious, it was no good looking like a new romantic when hip-hop was the flavour of the day. Choosing the *right* thing was difficult again because fashion and taste had always eluded me. I was the original teenager who had always been happy having his

Mother pick his clothes out from BHS. However, after much shopping deliberation I settled for a waistcoat with matching granddad shirt under the careful tutelage of a rather helpful shop assistant with an earring through her nose. I didn't usually subscribe to this type of interaction but in light of the situation I thought it best to get the advice of another female who wasn't my Mother. I was going to leave her a tip right up until the closing moments when she concluded her chic advice with,'And If I were you I'd wash that greasy hair of yours and change the cheap after shave you're wearing, you smell like a whores armpit.'

It was a bit embarrassing because she said it rather loudly and everyone in the shop seemed to turn their heads and look my way. It could have been paranoia but I'm sure I could almost hear them saying, *'she's right you know, he has got greasy hair'* and, 'look at old chip pan head over there. My cheeks turned a brighter shade of red as I paid my money to the cheeky bitch behind the counter, customer service was as dead and buried in this country as pounds shillings and pence. I left the premises shortly afterwards.

I figured had the clothes, and all I needed now was the right smells, it was as simple as that! It did anger me though: all these years, *all these bloody years*, and I never guessed I had greasy hair. Worse still it took a spotty shop assistant with glasses to tell me. That's almost as bad as your form tutor taking you to one side and introducing you to the merits of personal hygiene, all that aside I'd still be a fool to do nothing about it. So swallowing my pride I pressed onwards to the abode of pregnancy kits and hair gel, nothing was going to get in the way of my romantic success this coming Thursday night.

Unfortunately the shop assistant at the chemists wasn't so helpful selling me a lavender deodorant and some rather dubious own label aftershave called 'Beast's Claw', not exactly cricket but that's Folkestone for you. If that's what you get for being honest and asking some advice on affairs of the heart, I won't do that again I thought. Tuesday came and went, and so did Wednesday. Bloody slowly too! Thursday morning I got up early checked my face for new spots and then rushed through the streets of Folkestone to pick up the tickets for the disco that evening.

The Leas Cliff hall at Folkestone was a grand old building that had been thankfully restored to its former glory due to a landslide that almost cast its foundations back to the sea. I guess insurance companies do pay out sometimes! Apart from its fine Victorian architecture and gorgeous red drapes the 'Leas Cliff' was blessed with loads of little balconies and boxes, ideal for the odd hidden kiss or smooch. I tried to keep these thoughts out of my head because I was a gentleman at heart, but everytime I thought of Carla Dagostini they just crept back in. However, before that moment could come I'd have to first take care of my appearance. Shaving, spot squeezing and eyebrow plucking are a trio of duties that await the eager chaperone, three of the many duties that guarantee romantic success. I knew how important this was when I came across an old issue Jackie which read that men with eyebrows joining in the middle are more likely to have a violent disposition then those who don't. At fifteen I was humble enough not to question the experts so I plucked the little buggers out. Now Carla could look in my eyes and see the most passive man in the world, and sleep comfortably knowing I was no hurry to get a quick grope. The shaving wasn't so easy though: it's amazing how much blood can pour from a shaving nick, even more amazing was the pain of 'Beast's Claw' as it touched my skin. In the huge scale of things I guess men had shaving and women had periods however, in my Grandmothers case she had both tasks to deal with. Local legend says, that the bearded lady from Eltham could give any child from fifty yards a shaving rash with one of her kisses.

After the pain and pleasure of preening myself I practised snappy one liners in front of the mirror for an hour, but that *still* only took me round to four o'clock! I brushed my teeth and flossed again, this time doing each tooth individually, the clock now read four fifteen. Good. I had an hour and forty-five minutes to invest before leaving the house. The time *was* thankfully creeping on, but everytime it did so the butterflies in my stomach erupted in a fluttering orgy, and I worried if I'd remembered everything. Visually I was okay, I wasn't too preoccupied with the crease wrinkles in my shirt, my main worry concerned itself with the meeting of her clan. I'd seen enough television to know that things could go horribly wrong around family introductions. I mean, what *was* the correct etiquette in a situation like this, should I shake hands or kiss their rings? (Maybe I should re-phrase that) Surely It couldn't be that difficult, I'd just be polite, you know, complementary, but not too 'ass kissy'. I'd be confident too, but *not* 'cocky'. I wanted her parents to think they could trust me not fear me.

Swearing was of course a no, no, but slang was permissible, someone hip and trendy would keep their daughter on her toes. I checked my watch, no going back now it was time to go.

The Dagostini's front door bell played the Italian national anthem, I then realised I was in trouble. By the time I had reached the lounge I had been kissed by every woman in the house and frowned upon by all the men. I tried making pleasant eye contact with her parents, but they just stared straight through me in that Mafioso way. You know the look I'm talking about, the look that tells you they'll rip your heart out if you as much as breathe in their daughters ear, it was a great form of contraception I can tell you. As I spoke from Auntie's to cousins and then back to Auntie's again I tried to look on the whole circus as a group of people welcoming me to their family, but as the questions intensified it began to resemble a firing squad.

'Are you Catholic? Have you been confirmed? Do you believe in the Virgin Mary?

What does your Mother do? Really, does she play bridge?'

This was bearable.

'What are your plans for the future? Have you had sex yet? How many girlfriends have you had?'

Was not. It's not easy telling one lie after another, by the time I'd finished I was exhausted but happy because they'd all seemed to relax a bit, confident I would be joining the priesthood at sometime in the near future. Carla entered the room to a chorus of 'ahhh', she looked stunning in her black skirt and blue top.

'You're very early.'

'I didn't want to be late.'

Everyone laughed and I wondered why I said stupid things, why couldn't I have said something cool instead of stating the bloody obvious. Carla greeted everyone individually in Italian, picked up her handbag and whispered to me,

'Mind if we go now?'

'We've got plenty of time.'

She huffed impatiently.

'I know that, but if we spend another five minutes here my Mum will bring out the baby photo's.'

I loved my parents but they too could be embarrassing, with them it was food. They loved to see people eat, it didn't matter if you had an ass the size of the Milky Way, in my parents eyes everyone was thin and hungry. From the moment anyone entered the house to the moment they left, they were fed, even the dog hated walking it played havoc with her gout.

'Okay, we can go for a coffee or something.'

She smiled.

'Coffee would be great.'

So we said our good-byes and zigzagged out of the house much to the disappointment of the kissing relatives who were busy wailing in a typically Italian manner.

'Are you okay?'

She asked.

'Fine, shall we get that coffee now?'

'Yeah let's do that, and I'm sorry about my family, it's kind of traditional you see.'

I smiled.

'No problem at all.'

She looked quite hassled by the whole family introduction thing, probably feeling it was way too intense for a first date, but it didn't bother me. I was just happy to be here, gazing at the bumps in her blue top bobbing up and down as we made our way to Morelli's coffee shop. Lucky bra I thought.

The Leas Cliff Hall in all its majestic beauty loomed up in front of us. For the next two hundred and forty minutes its beautiful white outline would represent palace or prison. Things up until this point had gone very well, I'd shown initiative in my appearance, courtesy to family and empathy to Carla's culture now it was time to go in for the kill. Carla looked at me and smiled.

'I can't wait to get inside, all my friends are inside.'

I winced pulling one of those faces that shows visible disappointment, what did she mean, 'friends!' I wanted this night to be an intimate affair where we could talk, share a drink and maybe have a dance or two, how could I do that if I was on my own half the night waving to her from across the other side of the hall?

'So who are these friends?'

'Oh you'll love them, there's Bob, Paul, Simon, Peter and of course there's Johnny, you'll have to meet him, he's an absolute Romeo.'

Great! There was me thinking I'd be competing with a few 'fritzy-ditzy' grammar school girls for her attentions and now I find I'm competing with a roomful of men. My 'evens-on' bet had just had its odds slashed to a measly five to one, however my sense of worth never faltered. I wasn't prepared to show my disappointment openly, that would give her too much power early on.

'I can't wait to meet them.' I said through gritted teeth.

'I'm sure they're lovely.'

I know I had no right to be possessive of Carla's attentions but that kind of logic never enters a young boy's head. To quote Freddie Mercury, 'We want it all, and we want it now' and I was no different to the rest of the male race in that sense. You see, compromise and sharing are things that very few men ever learn, let alone fifteen-year old boys.

We passed through the glass doors of the Leas Cliff Hall our tickets pressed firmly into our palms. Entering into such a place laden with fake red roses and inflatable love hearts was an experience that took your breath away. After the usual pleasantries we made our way to the bar.

'Can I get you a drink?'

Carla thought for a minute excited at all the choices sitting on the top shelf.

'What are you having?'

'Oh, I'm only having a Coke, I'm not allowed anything else whilst I'm in training.'

An awkward moment of choosing unfolded, I could see Carla desperately wanted to taste the forbidden pleasures that her parents drunk, but she knew it wouldn't be good manners to do so if I was on cola. I bet 'Johnny Handsome' drank beer, I bet he drunk it by the lorry load I thought.

'I'll have a Coke too then.'

I wished I wasn't in training because I'd buy her the biggest lager and lime in the world and share it with her, but if my Father caught the slightest whiff of beer on my breath he'd kill me. I could hear it now, he'd give me the lecture on how, 'boxing and beer doesn't mix', and tell me the story of how Uncle Pat was pulled from a fight for having consumed a beer during training. It just wasn't worth it.

'You can have something else if you wish, just because I'm on cola doesn't mean you have to suffer too.'

Carla stuck to her guns and played the martyr.

'No Coke's fine.'

I turned and made my way to the bar while Carla rushed off to say hello to the whole world and his Mother, I didn't see her for a whole hour after that. It wasn't worth looking for her in a place the size of the Leas Cliff Hall either, we would have just been ships in the night, and I would have looked far too desperate. So I sat there with two glasses of Coke on my own, having finally understood the true soul meaning of every country and western song ever written. Loads of things went through my mind during that hour, the kind of self doubting thoughts that you don't usually like to challenge when you're on your own, and it was no good trying to change the course of my thoughts either. Everytime I did, I'd look down and see the two drinks sitting on there own and realise what a sad git I'd become. I wanted to get up and walk away in disgust but something kept me there glued to the seat. I chewed ice cubes and played 'beer-mat-voodoo' to pass the time because it's difficult to keep yourself amused while everyone else around is having such a good time. Should I stay and wait for the elusive Carla, or should I leave and save an inch of dignity for mankind? It was a tough call. Luckily I swallowed my pride with Carla coming back an hour and thirty minutes later full of apologies and affection.

'I'm *so* sorry.'

'No apologies between friends or lovers.'

I had heard Tom Cruise use this line in 'Top Gun' and it kind of fitted the moment perfectly, Carla looked confused though.

'Now how about that beer?'

Carla looked shocked.

'What about your training?'

'To hell with it, there's more important things in life than boxing, now can I get you that drink?'

She smiled, and I completely forgot about the negative feelings of an hour before.

'Okay, I'll have a large Dram and Coke.'

'*A large Dram and Coke*'! Who did she think she was going out with? I wasn't made of money, I was hoping she'd have half a lager and lime, or a pint of lager top at best, not a bloody liqueur from some banana growing republic.

'Coming right up.'

I returned to the bar happier than before because the odds were once again swaying in my favour, at least I wouldn't be sharing this drink alone.

'What'll be mate?'

'A pint of lager, and a large Dram and Coke.'

The barman paused the way they do when they are weighing up a situation. The next sixty seconds would be crucial because we *both* knew I wasn't eighteen, but how handled the transaction from this point onwards would determine whether I purchased my goods or not.

'Have you got any I.D. on you?'

I couldn't go back to the delectable Carla with yet another glass of cola, I really would be spending the rest of the night on my own. I had to think quick, hesitation on my part would give the game away. So I looked the barman straight between the eyes and with all the confidence of a warrior and said.

'You don't need to see my identification.'

The force was with me, I may have plagiarised Obi Wan but I did it with all the bravery of a Jedi Knight, and I didn't even possess a light sabre.

There was a silent second, the barman frowned taking in all of my statistics before making a decision and smiling.

'Okay, but if anyone asks you're eighteen.'

I took the drinks back to the table and felt grown up for the first time in my life, being able to buy drinks at public bars seemed to help me walk that little bit taller and right now I was about six foot two.

'One large Dram and Coke, and a pint of lager for me.'

I took a sip, and that's when the guilt kicked in. What the hell was my Father going to say, worse than that how was he going to feel? All the support he gave me with the endless nights at the gym and at the park. All the money he'd scraped together to get me to all the various shows, I'd really let him down. This was not the way a future champ was supposed to act, to quote Sylvester Stallone in Rocky, 'women weaken legs', *and it was bloody true*! I put the put the pint of poison down with a bang.

'What's a matter?'

'I can't do this.'

It came out worse than I wanted it to.

'I mean, I can't drink this lager. I know it sounds stupid, but I feel I would be letting my Father down. You see, I promised him I wouldn't.'

Carla looked at me admiringly and I felt embarrassed.

'It's not stupid, it's nice that you care.'

She put her drink down and smiled.

'You don't think I'm being silly?'

'Not at all.'

The music in the background swelled filling the room, Carla looked me, and I looked right back. She hadn't looked at me that way before, I liked it, but what did it mean? Do I lean across and kiss her now, or do I play it frosty? She cupped her hands and took a small sip of Drambuie from the glass, she was obviously undecided too. I'm not too old to remember the excitement of these, 'shall I?' moments, the ones where you don't know what to do next, it's what growing up is all about. Should I suggest something, a dance perhaps, or should I wait for her feminine suggestion? She looked at me again, so I looked right back, we couldn't carry on like this in silence one of us would get bored, and then what?

'Fancy a wander?'

'A wander where?'

'Oh just round the hall, maybe you can introduce me to some of those friends of yours.'

Carla screwed her face up, I'd been forward too early. Maybe she thought I only had carnal sin on my mind, maybe she thought I just wanted to get her up in the balconies for some 'hanky-panky' and dirty talk. I was such an idiot. Her hesitation at saying 'okay' held my confidence in limbo as she weighed up all the options but when she did say yes, I wanted to sing from the highest buildings in the town. I wanted to tell the whole world that I was in love with a woman called Carla and that one day she would love me too.

We made our way up to the balconies and looked at all the people below bobbing and swaying to the music. Carla slipped her hand into mine and the moment was crowned by the DJ who commenced the 'slowies' with Brian Hyland singing 'Sealed With a Kiss'. She looked at me again, but this time I acted by running my fingertips through her hair and doing what I had been dying to do for months. I kissed her. I kissed her with every breath that was me, exposing myself giving everything, prepared to receive nothing. Pressing her lips to mine touched every part of my body and up until that day I had never kissed anyone like that. I suppose that when I think about it, I realise that the whole thing from beginning to end couldn't have lasted more than ten seconds, but regardless of this, it still represents the 'cherry high' moment of my adolescence. The brief moments we shared that night and shortly afterwards will always remain a warm place as I look back and whenever she is I'd like to say thank-you.

CHAPTER 3
Mr. Self Destruct

Mr. Self Destruct your life is now defunct,
You picked your wars and now you've lost,
Time to weigh the obscene cost.
You smoked the pot and guzzled the wines,
Fought with women ignored the signs.
It's time to rest and time to change,
Time to extend your shallow range.
You reap what you sow,
And eat what you know,
Don't you think it's time to rest?

I didn't telephone my parents for a whole month when I moved out of the marital home and I instructed them to do the same, I wanted to be isolated. It sounds mercenary but the last thing I wanted was nurturing, it would just made me feel guilty. Yes, I knew my parents were worried, but I didn't care, for that first month I was totally immersed in getting myself together and I couldn't do that if they were fussing around. You see, I needed time to heal, and I instinctively knew that I had to do that on my own. I'd always had supportive people around me and *that* I think was part of the problem, I didn't think I could cut it on my own anymore, but I'd never know that for sure unless I started severing some of these ties. I know some people reading this will see me as a typical Garbo-esc character saying, *'I want to be left alone'*, but it wasn't like that, it wasn't like that at all.

On the first week of moving in I painted my room. This isn't something that I usually like to pay a lot of attention to, but this time it was different. I wanted it to feel right, something grounding in case I lost it in the middle of the night. After much debate and mixing I settled for a colour called 'patio rainforest', a nice little mixture that I slapped onto the walls with gusto, painting everything from top to bottom apart from a little patch above the door. On this canvas I scratched the words, 'everything dies', I did this to remind myself that things were always on the move, and that nothing lasts forever. On reflection it smacks of *teenage angst*, but because I couldn't think of anything smarter to say it has stayed there. I really hate this time in my life, I know endings happen but I don't like them because they remind me I'm mortal. In this sense I'm probably not that different to the rest of the human race because our socialisation prepares us for everything except death, this is good learning but doesn't help me in the dark when everyone's gone to bed. It's scary because I've thought about this a lot, believing that death is the ultimate metaphor for all endings, and this thought humbles me into child mode where I remember that as people we don't really control anything. Not helpless in ourselves but in the fragility of our lives. Yes, we can place certain secure things around us, but ultimately we can be taken at anytime by illness or accident. I know that everyone has this concern but how many people ever say it out loud or better still put it down in black and white?

    My main preoccupation at the moment is the fear that I won't achieve inner peace, and how can I when I constantly move round in huge ugly circles? I see it in cartoon fashion like the 'wacky races' but in this race I'm not dashing for the finishing line I'm running from it, running away from my shadow self because I don't want to confront anything. It's strange though because I *do* want to reach the finishing line, I want an ending so I can bring these two people together. I'm pissed off with the schizophrenic bullshit of being two people, that's where my indecision comes from: I can't choose between either one, you see, the real me and the shadow me are in conflict but they are both of the same person. The ending of my marriage hurt more than anyone will ever know not just because I loved my wife with all my heart, but because it extenuated the gap between my 'selves'. I know what I want , but I don't know if I'll ever be able to have it in the present climate. So, if anyone out there has a magic wand please grant the following.

I want to be myself, in one world doing what I want to. I want to belong to something and I also want independence. Most of all I want permission to be myself without hurting anyone else and without feeling guilt. If I could just be oblivious to everything, like some of the people I'd met, life would be easier.

My Mate Johnny

Friends are important, but flawed friends are more interesting. With flawed friends we have endless miles of discussion; money they've lost, stupid advice they've given and countless fights they've supposedly won. Strange, but without flawed friends we would never have anybody to laugh at. Take for instance my friend John Ashwood, ever met an unfortunate character with a self-destruct button? Well let me tell you about him.

John's parent's Doug and Mary were settled traveller's, gypsies who'd managed to make their money in the hedgehog pie business before retiring in their late thirties. By traveller standards I suppose they had done quite well, a house, a car and a dog, all paid for by the time they were both thirty-nine, who said yuppies had to work in the city? So, there they were, 52 Linden Road Coxheath, thirty-nine and everything paid for. Couples who reach this stage in life so early often seek full time hobbies like hiking or boat building, but not the Ashwood's. The Ashwood's were traditional people so they done the next best thing to keep the boredom away, they expanded their tribe. That's right, John and Mary Ashwood took the decision to have kids at the ripe old age of thirty-nine feeling that they had something positive to offer a next generation. Douglas JNR was the first to come along, and then eighteen months later Mary gave birth to John. A difficult birth that lasted a total of twenty-six hours exhausting both the staff and the hospital drug supply. Mary was a rock though, joking that she hadn't been so high in *at least* ten days. It was this, and her combined love of imperial maths that kept her going. At current market value she estimated that she'd had at least fifty quid's worth (Drugs) in the last twenty-four hours, like I say, 'a rock'.

  The boys grew up hand in hand, Douglas took to Lego construction and John took to demolition. When John reached the terrible two's and the volume of the homestead increased to a level that contravened current European guidelines Douglas SNR took a job at the local brewery. This left poor Mary alone to deal with an angelic Douglas JNR and a demonic mutant called John who had now taken to urinating in every room of the house except the toilet. At breakfast times when Douglas JNR could be seen eating his porridge nicely and John could be seen throwing his up the wall, Mary would think. Wonder if John was possibly someone else's child, swapped by a freak accident in the maternity ward two years previous. I mean he didn't look like his brother. Doug was tall and dark with chiselled charms, whereas poor john was short and squat with rodent like features, a face only a Mother could love.

The local primary school was only round the corner so when Douglas JNR reached five he was able to walk there unattended daily by his Mother or Father. He liked this, it made him feel grown up like the big boys at the junior school, they *also* walked to school without their parents. John on the other hand who was four at the time wasn't so content with the situation. He felt that Douglas JNR's daily walk to school was a security risk to the existence of the clan. So out of love more than anything else John would escort Douglas JNR. To and fro school complete with a cricket bat in his hand. Anyone who said anything derogatory or frowned at his brother in anyway were struck on the cranium with the bat. So when John Ashwood joined the school some eighteen months later he already had a fearful reputation. Despite his three-foot stature John Ashwood was the type of child who was given a wide birth by everyone. This was sad because little John was just reaching out, the fact that he was reaching out with a cricket bat made it slightly more difficult for the other children to get to know him though. This didn't bother John at first, he enjoyed the fact that he was respected from afar, being feared meant he was never asked by the other kids to share his sweets or milk. It's a minor thing I know, but in a world where sweets and milk are the only currency it looked like a good position to be in. However, in the words of Lou Reed, ' You reap what you sow', and when the birthday circuit worked it's way around not one invite came John's way. This was hardly surprising because in John's race to become Reggie Kray he had isolated himself from the other kids in the class. He was a tough kid, being sent to Coventry was just one measure of his toughness and to the outside world John's denial was complete. A bad boy, a rebel without a cause, and whatever you do don't invite him to your party. Sadly John would repeat this pattern time after time in his life always at his own expense. I don't know why he was so anti-social because deep down he was a very lonely person. The only thing I can put it down to is that John secretly wanted to be Douglas SNR. He scorned his popularity and despised the way the teachers always chanted his Brothers name, it seemed Douglas JNR would always tower above him. Worse still was the fact that these feelings were allowed to fester until they grew into something ugly that psychologists call 'displacement'. This is where an individual can project his/her inward anger at themselves, or outwards onto others for no other reason than them being there. So, in the first twenty-one years of his life through no conscious effort he managed to hit, upset or threaten just about everyone in the village, his popularity was capped at the age of seventeen when he also developed a strong liking for cider and blackcurrant. John Ashwood had no friends except me, but even our friendship had its limits.

At the age of twenty-two John fell in love with a black prostitute called Jenny, why? I don't know, because John was the most jealous man in the world.

Previous history had seen him loose his temper uncontrollably if his girlfriends so much as looked at another man, how was he going to deal with Jenny's occupation? I asked him this, and John being John just shrugged his shoulders and said. 'You can't help who you fall in love with.'

This I suppose was true but wasn't the kind of thing that I expected to hear from John's lips, maybe on daytime television but never from the lips of a settled gypsy.

'Doesn't it bother you that she sleeps with other men?'

Whenever I asked John this John would pat my back reassuringly and say,

'It's just a job, and to be honest I don't ask about it.'

This statement would have been lovely if it was true but it wasn't, John's jealousy was as strong as ever. As soon as Jenny finished her shift he would be straight on the phone asking her explicit details about the men she had slept with. How good they were, how long they lasted, and were they better than him? It was a crazy situation in which he had no right to ask questions, remember, John had always known that Jenny was a lady of the night right from the start. This logic didn't seem to cross his mind and in that way he was an incredibly selfish man, any argument that he'd ever had was always about himself and *his* feelings. Not once had I ever heard him self reflect or except the consequences of his actions, and this relationship was no different. So they argued and they bickered, they split up, and they got back together again all over a period of six months until one day when Jenny had had enough. She didn't need this, her life was difficult as it was. She had gone out with John on the back of having a good time and now all he did was make her miserable, Jenny had wanted a boyfriend not another pimp.

So bright one October morning after a particularly heavy night Jenny got up and packed what stuff she could while John still lay half unconscious, he had used his hands on her once too often and now it was time to go. No tears and no dear John letter, Jenny was leaving. To me or you the contemplation of leaving a partner would prove to be a heart wrenching experience, but for Jenny it was nothing, a woman like her was always on the move shedding a skin before creating another. First the bedroom for her clothes, then the bathroom for her toiletries. Her emotionless face gave nothing away, her packing as methodical as making a cup of tea or rolling a cigarette. In fifteen minutes she was finished, and her world was mobile once again. She zipped her last hold-all bag up and left through the front door *never* looking back, she had concluded this chapter of her life.

John got up at about one in the afternoon with a stinking hangover, as he rose from his pit he called Jenny's name and silence was his reply. Maybe she hadn't heard him, so he called her again and just like before, nothing. John didn't like it, something was wrong, Jenny was always there when he got up. It was one of those silent rules that every relationship has, and now it had been broken. A fleeting flashback swept across his mind as he remembered a confrontation followed by a fight, he winced. What manner of punishment had he bestowed upon her this time? God he could be so stupid.

He stood up from the floor mattress and tip-toed through the broken glass that showered the bedroom, he was almost too scared to leave the room for he wasn't sure what he'd find. The morning after with all of its black spots made him paranoid, because under the influence he was never in control.

'Jenny'

He shouted almost wishing her there, but he knew she was gone. This time he had pushed the boat out too far, the lights were out and the heating was off, and Jenny was nowhere to be seen. It was over, and what's more it was all his fault. John froze and looked the scene, tears swelled in his eyes stinging his face as they ran down his cheeks. Once again he had taken something holy and raped it to shit, destroying his comfort with spite, the behaviour of all alcoholics and madmen.

He looked at the time and surmised that she couldn't have left that long before him. Maybe if he found her and apologised he could talk her back into a reconciliation. John picked up the telephone book in the hallway with all its little scratched numbers on the cover, Jenny may have left but she was also a creature of habit. Whenever she was in-between places she would return to the one place that she felt safe, the place where she stashed all of her money, her step-Father's house. John quickly tapped out the number, thank God the phone hadn't been cut off as well.

'Hello'

The voice of her step-Father said.

'Hello, could I speak to Jenny if she's there.'

There was an uncomfortable pause.
'Is that John?'
'Yes.'

He didn't need to hear what was coming but he let the old man have his say just the same.

'She's told me that she doesn't want anything to do with you John, so take my advice and stay away eh.'

The words weren't threatening but they *were* firm, this was a man who'd seen his step-Daughter taken advantage of by one man or another all of her life so he knew the score.

'I only wanted a quick word.'

Her step-Father sighed on the other end of the telephone.

'I've already told you John, that's *not* going to be possible.'

It was weird because John usually flew into a rage upon hearing the word 'no' but it was very difficult to get into a confrontation with a man like her step-Father who sounded so confidently chilled on the other end of the phone.

'I only wanted to say I was sorry.'

'Look, I'm not a messenger. Sorry or not, she still doesn't want to speak to you. Now don't call here again, okay.'

John screamed down the line but it was too late because he'd already hung up. If he wanted to talk to her, then he would regardless of his step-Father's calming aura. He grabbed his coat and a quart of Vodka and then made his way to her house on the other side of town. It might cause trouble but she couldn't put the phone down on him if he turned up on her doorstep could she? If he chose his words carefully he might even be granted an audience with the scarlet woman who he'd fallen in love with.

'Let me in!'

John punched the front door.

'I want to talk to you, *let me in I said.*'

Inside the house footsteps passed up and down the passageway as everyone inside contemplated their next move. John may have been small but with the vodka inside him he was a giant. Jenny knew John's temper best so she came to the door first.

'John go home, it's over.'

'Not until we've spoken about it face to face. I want to say I'm sorry, doesn't that mean anything to you?'

It didn't, she was finished with his apologies. 'Sorry' was a lovely word that ran thin on the ground when the same mistakes were made time and time again.

'Okay you're sorry but that doesn't change a thing, now go home!'.

There it was again, that bloody 'no' word with all of its damn restrictions, he'd take it on a good day from a stranger but he'd never take it off her with all of her bloody airs and graces. He hit the front door a final time with his fist and then walked back down the path, picked the iron gate from its hinges, and threw it through the front window. The noise was colossal as the glass showered the window seal and the lounge inside. Jenny's step-Father who had been watching from the same lounge stood in shock for a second, surveying the mess that decorated the carpet in his newly decorated room.

I told you I'd talk face to face with you.'

John sneered through the window to Jenny who had now joined her step-Father.

'Right, that's it.'

Jenny's step-Father rolled his sleeves up, picked up a random piece of timber broken off from the window frame and climbed through to get at John.

'You're going to pay for that you little shit.'

All of a sudden the Dutch courage from the vodka ran dry, as strong as John's five foot frame was, it was still no match for the strapping width of Jenny's step-Father. Out of fight, plight and fright John chose to run, I guess at heart all bullies are cowards.

'Come here and take what's coming to you.'

Were the last words John was to hear as he sprinted round the corner eager to put as much distance between him and the house, but as he ran he fell twisting his ankle. The pain was excruciating and plight was now no longer an option and neither was catching the bus. John needed a plan 'B' and quick. Then he saw it, right there in front of him like a big shimmering mirage promising life and salvation. Just ten yards across the road lay an ambulance station full of open vehicles with keys in the ignition. If he could just borrow one temporarily, he could secure his escape, avoid a beating, and contemplate his next move with nobody being the wiser.

John got back to his feet and hobbled across the road just as Jenny's step-Father trotted round the corner.

'Oi, where do you think you're going?'

Time was up, it was grand theft auto or grandslam wrestling, an easy choice to make when you're being chased by a hairy gorilla with GBH on his mind. John ran straight for the nearest ambulance and sped out of the depot with Jenny's step-Father in close pursuit like Mel Gibson in Lethal Weapon. It was nice to getaway but he knew he was in real trouble now. When you take the decision to throw an iron gate through someone's front window and then steal an ambulance, *you know* that sooner or later you're going to have to answer to someone. John didn't care though, John was now Steve McQueen racing away from Nazi occupation in a vehicle designed for escape.

'You little bastard, come back!'

John stuck his hand out the window and raised his middle finger in the air, a physical statement designed to infuriate his pursuer, who had now worked up quite a sweat in the rear view mirror. Round the corner he swung the vehicle hitting close to fifty miles an hour on a rather difficult bend by Benneton, the ambulance grumbled but John kept his line of angle. He had to get out of town quickly because a white van with 'paramedic' tattooed on it's side wasn't something that blended into the surroundings, but it was difficult. Traffic was heavy, and pedestrians constantly hampered his efforts to move the jalopy up into fourth gear. He didn't like dramatics but if wanted to get this vehicle through town quickly he'd have to turn the siren on. For a split second he took his eyes off the road to look for the switch that would kick start that awful whining sound, and that's when disaster struck. Just as he flipped the switch a child ran out in front of the cab making John slam on the breaks. Grand theft auto was one thing but manslaughter was a completely different ball park. The ambulance skidded and then veered uncontrollably to the left as John span the steering wheel furiously to gain control. The child was safely out of the way now but he ambulance was heading for a collision with the brick wall that surrounded Woolworth's.

The sound of metal and shattering brick stopped everybody in their tracks, the ambulance which was supposed to be the ultimate thing in safe travel crumbled and fell apart, demolition derby had nothing on John Ashwood's driving skills. John was actually thankful to be drunk this time because it numbed the pain from a gash on his forehead that ran from one side of his face to the other, vodka did have its advantages. John fell out of the drivers seat, he was lucky to be alive, *so very lucky*. He wiped the blood from his forehead that was running into his eyes blinding him, and staggered along the side of the vehicle to the back doors that had swung open during the accident. A crowd had gathered now at the back of the destroyed mess that once had represented the white angel of the emergency services. This annoyed John because not one member of the public approached him to ask if *he* was okay, they seemed more concerned with the back of the vehicle. You should have seen them, they were like bloody flies hovering over shit, all pointing and gossiping like stinky old ladies discussing the price of luncheon meat.

John was going to leave the scene of the crime as quick as he could to avoid accommodation at the blue lamp hotel but his interest had been pricked by the crowd. So he pushed his way to the front to see what they were all talking about. As he pulled the ambulance doors apart his heart sank. Inside the vehicle sitting in shock sat a doctor, a nurse, and a patient, the three of them had been waiting to be taken home as part of the NHS charter.

'There he is.'

The angry crowd shouted.

'There's the bastard.'

John started to back up, to be hung drawn and quartered by a bunch of pissy OAP's was more frightening than being arrested by the Police.

'I bet he's an agency driver.'

Shouted one old man.

'Somebody call the Police'.

Said another. There must have been at least twenty witnesses all of them prepared to make a statement in his conviction.

'It's not what you think.'

John stammered.

'I was just trying to get home.'

'But you didn't need to crash into Woolworth's, what have they ever done to you?' Said a loyal old lady concerned that the cost of the accident would increase the price of the pick and mix counter inside.

'I didn't mean it.'

'Tell that to the Police.'

To reason at this stage was futile. He forgot about his aches and pains, forgot about the gash on his forehead and forgot about the mad step-Father who wanted his blood. He had to get away before the crowd became organised and held him, so for the second time that day John ran. Ran like a rabbit, ran like a leopard and ran like a coward all the way to my house. I don't know what he expected me to do, I was hardly able to afford petrol for my car let alone organise a new identity in a different country, but all the same I patched him up and got him a cup of tea.

'Why don't you give yourself up John?'

The very words sounded like something out of a movie, the kind of thing that Paul Newman would have said to a wanted man contemplating suicide.

'They'll catch up with you sooner or later, you know that don't you? Come on, maybe they'll give you a break.'

John's face took on a look of disgust, it seemed as if everyone was against him even his best friend. It was alright for people like me, I wouldn't have to deal with four drab walls and food that wasn't fit for a dog. John moved in closer so I could smell his vodka breath.

'I'm not giving myself up, I came here to escape.'

Great plan John, two miles away from the crime scene and my parents due home from work in ten minutes.

'You can't stay here.'

'I know that, I need money so I can getaway.'

I was frightened to ask anymore but my silence wouldn't stay dormant.

'Where do you plan on going?'

'France.'

He snapped back,

'And I want you to take me there.'

Great, here I am with eight pounds sixty-three in my pocket and half a tank of petrol stuck in a ford Orion with bald tires, and this wanker wants me to take him to France.

'John, I'll help in whatever way I can, but I don't have the money to get you to France.'

John sucked his lips and thought,

'What about Hastings?'

I thought about the money and then thought about the petrol, there was still eleven days until pay-day. If I took the car to Hastings I wouldn't have the funds to return.

'What about Hawkhurst, it's the best I can do? You can hitch the other twelve miles.'

'Done.'

So that's what I did. I dropped John and his problems at Hawkhurst High Street and returned home. To this day I still don't know what happened to him or even if he's alive, but wherever he is I wish him luck, the crazy bastard.

CHAPTER 4
New Horizons

I used to feel so big,
Untouchable, invincible.
Confident and unafraid of change.
Willing and zestful at the moving forward.
Embracing with both arms the warmth of new horizons.
That was before.
Before you, before this.
Before the tears of disappointment.
Before the lies and deceptions of failures.
Embracing with both arms the warmth of new horizons.

I rigged a mirror up in my bedroom, nothing flash, just a small thing to sit by the door. Some of my superstitious friends have told me that mirrors in bedrooms are not a good idea, apparently they project the soul inwards. It's nice that they care enough to mention it but I don't think I'll let it bother me, the mirror can stay, maybe I'll learn a thing or two as I implode. Or maybe I'll place my overdraft in front of the mirror and project it back into the black, who knows. Advice like this I love, it's replaced small talk, two things I don't seem to engage in anymore. This wasn't always the case, there was time not so long ago that I listened to *all* the advice I could get. I thought advice came from experience and that this experience would help me project myself better, a bit like combing my appearance in a mirror. I look at the lines on my face now and realise what a crock of shit this is. All this advice and knowledge never helped me save my marriage, it just prolonged the agony. If I'd listened to myself right at the beginning I don't think I'd be having the kind of self doubts I do today.

People have laughed at me leaving work and going back to education, they ask me what I'm trying to prove as if it's some mid-life crisis. They ask me if there's any chance of Karen and I getting back together, these people I have now isolated from my life. Do they really think I'd go through this much pain if there was another option? I left work because I was fed up of my white collar reflection, and I didn't particularly fancy having the next sixty years of my life tied to some damn job description. The simple truth is, that when things started going wrong between Karen and I wanted to change everything. So when I look in the little mirror now, I may not be happy with the sad man who stares back at me, but at least I know there's honesty in his eyes. Maybe I'm flawed but I'm no different to the rest of the human race.

My Mother

My Mother's story is a complicated one that is not always understood by outsiders, I'm not critical of this because empathy is a quality that we all struggle with from time to time. As amateur voyeurs we only see the aftermath of experience, the behaviour that manifests itself in the form of weird and wonderful habits, often pissing us off or making us nervous.

My Mum was brought up in a dirty little London borough called Depford. (This is not meant to offend anyone) She lived with her Mum, Dad, Brother and two Grandmothers in a big house on the main road. Materialistically, she had a great life: holiday's every year, clean clothes and good food, but emotionally her life was as troubled as Beirut on a bad day: blackmail, guilt and ritual beatings. The challenging quandary about my Mum's situation was not the lack of love but the quantity of abuse that went on behind closed doors, but to explain this I'll have to describe her significant family members one by one starting with her Grandmother.

This lady was a mean callous authoritarian, you can always spot them, they're the ones who *never* smile in family photographs and remain bitterly antagonist towards the milkman, but at first glance you may have thought something else. Looking at my Mother's Grandmother her you would have seen a well-educated smart woman with all the airs and graces of an 1930's uptown girl. She had a good command of English, and a good knowledge of all those middle class niceties that seem to sit so smugly next to the plumbs in their mouths, but the reality was quite different. Those who knew her feared her because this woman was a secret nazi general who commanded her troops with the 'Bond-esc' motto 'failure is not tolerated'. When she gave an order, she expected it to be carried out, and without question too! Dereliction of duties resulted in punishment, usually administered by one of her drill sergeants. When she couldn't get what she wanted she engaged in the age old London tactic of 'throwing a wobbly' or in her case, a fake dramatic diabetes fit brought on by stress. This regressive act would serve as a reminder to everyone in the house that she was still boss, and God help anyone who forgot it! Everybody knew that she didn't suffer with diabetes but that didn't stop them all running around trying to find the old dear some sugar when she was foaming from the mouth and barking at everyone like a rabid dog. When the fit subsided everyone barring my Mum (Who was cynical from an early age) would crowd around to comfort her, it was like a scene out of the bloody 'Walton's' but with none of the sincerity.

'Whatever's that matter?'

Would sound from the front line, it was so rehearsed it was sickening. They might as well have said, *'We're bored too, let's beat Sylvie'* at least it would have been more honest.

'Whose upset you?'

Would be the next battle cry, and then in-between crocodile tears and sniffs the old battleaxe would exact her spite on my Mum. Not because she was naughty or anything, but just because she could. My Mother didn't fit the mould because she didn't play the game and her Grandmother wanted her to know that in her little world there was no greater power than *she*.

'It was Sylvie, (sniff, sniff) she was being so naughty, (little whimper) and and...'

That was it! Out would come the carpet beater from the cupboard. Off would come her garments ripped or pulled it didn't matter. Then, in front of everyone she would be beaten, naked until she curled up into a little regressive ball on the floor. If this wasn't humiliating enough, in the middle of all the madness her Grandmother would exert a final piece of control by deciding how hard the final blows should be.

To describe my Mother's Brother is easy: a no good twisted pervert who shared the family's gene pool! Derrick loved nothing more than to inflict all manner of visual abuses on my Mother knowing that *he* lived in a consequence free environment. Derrick was the blue-eyed boy living outside of justice and fair play, two things he had little understanding of. To him, my Mother was a toy to be played with, a little inanimate object that belonged to the family and therefore belonged to him. She was worthless. If he wanted to be crude with her it was justified by the fact that he didn't have a girlfriend, and if he became violent it was merely assumed that my Mother had started it again.

Modern psychologists would term this dysfunctional but I can think of much more colourful descriptions if I put my mind to it. Derrick had all the outward power a young boy could want because he had sold his dignity out a long time ago, but none of the inward calm we all desire in order to exist a normal life, whatever that means.

Her Mother on the other hand (My Grandmother) had all the inward calm she thought she could handle, this was a woman who had made a career out of gaining control. The house was *her* world, and in her little ivory tower she could influence just about anything that went on in *that* house. Her abusive tactics were altogether more sinister though, my Grandmother's power was words. The things she would say, the way she would say them, and the things that could be implied from them. All of them like little seeds waiting to be watered in the eggshell mind of my Mother. She never liked getting her own hands dirty, why should she when she had my Grandfather as chief executioner? No, she liked words. Words that hurt, and words that bleached a child's confidence. She would sit my Mother of the floor of the kitchen, and tell her for hours on end that she was 'ugly' and 'wicked' and that no one would ever want to marry her. Over and over she'd hurl insults at her, imprinting these words in my mother's mind until they became *her* beliefs. If she had be born twenty years later I believe that the culmination of beatings, sexual abuse and emotional torment would have been enough to have placed her in care with a good foster family, but back in the 1960's she was stuck. Glued to that tiny piece of floor in the kitchen, enduring the rantings of a crazy woman 'hell-bent' on world domination.

My Mothers existence was hard because from a very early age she had an *awareness* that life at her house was not exactly normal. It would have been very easy for her to roll over like her Brother and become one with the family ethos, but she didn't. From about the age of seven she made a stand, nothing glamorous, but a pledge to keep her dignity. She *wouldn't* comply to her Mother's unreasonable demands anymore, and she *wouldn't* except her Brother's behaviour as normal. To make this stand was extremely brave because over the next thirteen years every family member tried to break her spirit with unspeakable acts of wickedness. Twenty years she lived there, two decades of repression, but she was never beaten and that's what hurt them I think. Despite all their power, the beatings, curfews and blackmail they just couldn't break my Mother. This wasn't because she was a superhuman with insurmountable powers or anything, she was just flesh and blood like the rest of us, her clinging to reality was by way of method. For in times of trouble my Mother would shut her mind off from the real world and place herself in a dream state, a fantasy-land that would become her reality, a place she could feel safe and content. In this land she had a little house with four

windows, a husband who loved her and two adoring children. You should have seen it! The downstairs of the house was taken up with a lounge and galley kitchen where copper pots and pans hung from the ceiling, whilst upstairs was a myriad of pastel colours and wall rugs. A strange fantasy you might say, but this is where she'd live locked safely away, whilst being prodded and poked by her parents and Brother. Just rocking back and forth, thinking of her husband children and the white picket fence that surrounded her make believe home. Sometimes she get into her dream so much that she'd hum little conversations under her breath,
nothing amazing just chit-chat, but this idle talk would make her grin like a Cheshire cat and they didn't like this either. To them this happiness was wrong because it undermined them by taking their power away, and that in their eyes was unacceptable, so the abuse would intensify. Belittlement, lines of clever insults and sexual abuse, all designed to feed my Mothers cancer of inadequacy.

    The trouble is, that when you live with this type of behaviour day in and day out you start to believe it. Sadly by the time my Mother had reached puberty she had gained a suitcase full of emotional hang-ups that had manifested themselves as a direct result of her upbringing. For my Mother it was food, 'food glorious food', the more the better. When she was feeling down or upset she would gorge herself for comfort. Sweet biscuits, crisps and chocolates it didn't matter what really, as long as she got that warm feeling in her belly. That contented tingle that starts in the stomach but resonates throughout the whole body as the system swallows up whatever it's being fed. It doesn't take a Mathematician to work out that her weight yo-yoed erratically throughout her teenage years.

As a small child when my Father had gone to work I would see the scars of her childhood reappear as the voices of her past reared their ugly heads in her mind. In my eyes she'd be alright, but then something *small* would happen.

It didn't have to be anything bad, it could be a bill she didn't really want to open, or an unwanted phone call from a friend, anything really. She deal with the situation as you'd expect any Mother to, and deal with it perfectly too, but in the process she'd get all quiet and glassy eyed. You see it was surprises she didn't like, things that came from out of nowhere and caught her off guard, decisions out of the blue that she had to make on her own is *what she didn't like.* Not all disturbances were bad of course, but the ones that *were* stressful seemed upset my Mother more than they would other people. 'Bad disturbances' like overdue bills would entail my Mother having to perform by making a decision, and decisions would place her in an environment she wouldn't feel safe in. Anytime a judgement call was needed my Mother wouldn't feel empowered like you would imagine her to be, instead she would feel panicky. 'Was she good enough?' 'Was she capable?' would sound through her head as the transference of her childhood experiences would make themselves present in the here and now. To outsiders she would deal with the 'bad disturbance' like an adult, saying all the right things with a smile on her face, but in her mind she was somewhere else. Mainly in the past, for people retreat under stress and in her heart she was still that little girl sitting on the kitchen floor being told how 'stupid' and 'wicked' she was.

After the event I would watch my Mother dunk packs of biscuits under the hot tap in the kitchen and consume them one after one. It was like she was in a race or something, I couldn't believe how much food she would eat. Then it would be onto the crisps and chocolate, and three or four hours later she would feel ill often complaining of a pain in her stomach. Growing up watching this I never really saw it as strange, I just gathered that this was what adults did when they were upset. I figured that because grown-ups were so much bigger than me, they must need more food to sustain themselves during times of trouble, it was as simple as that. Kids always have a wonderful way of breaking confusion down into its lowest common denominator. The truth was quite different of course because as irrational as it sometimes looked, the need of food had become a sanctuary to my Mother. It was a place where she gained comfort from feeling good, but only for a short time. Next would come the sheer gasps of panic when she hit the scales the following day. Her body would often have problems dealing with the sheer volumes of food it would have to digest with, so naturally she would retain water. On really bad days she could put on up to four pounds in weight and this would really freak her out. Times like this would involve a talk from my Mother where I'd be made to promise not to run errands for her to the sweet shop. I knew that these promises would only remain valid until the next craving or binge but I promised all the same. To not promise would be to fall out of favour with the woman who managed my pocket money fund.

Much later when life threw a set of difficult challenges in her path her addiction intensified with slimming tablets, and for a very short while she was to make herself extremely ill. I think it was during this low point that she actually found some clarity, some answers down in the dirt where she felt she was. She knew that if she continued destroying herself then her parents legacy would live on in the eyes of her children, and she didn't want that to happen. The turning point however was slightly more traumatic for my Mother.

We were living in Folkestone at the time running a little guesthouse in a street called Darby Road. It wasn't the nicest neighbourhood in the world but the writing material was way above average. We had an Irish man up the road called 'Casey' who would be busted every week for smoking dope. A lazy teenager across the road who refused to get out of his bed to urinate, and a couple of out of work Turkish 'lap-top' dancers running from violent husbands. The whole living experience was great but the greatest thing about living in a guesthouse on the coast was that we'd always get a lot of visitors. Uncles, Auntie's and Cousins, all looking for a cut price day at the seaside. Mum and Dad loved visitors especially children, and we did too because it was always a good way to wangle a trip to the fairground with my Mother.

I can't remember exactly when because time evades me, but somewhere around the spring of '82 we had a couple of visitors. Ian and Sue, two lifelong friends of my parents who had a little daughter called Kelly. It wasn't a planned visit, these things rarely are. They had just jumped in the car one Saturday morning and without thinking ended up at Folkestone in search of *'kiss me quick'* hats and candy floss. Dad was pleased, his beloved spaghetti bolognaise would now not go waste, and Mum was pleased too because she now had a child in the house to spoil. They had been there about an hour, the usual pleasantries were exchanged when the topic of a fairground trip was raised by my Sister. Penny was always first to ask for everything, a trait I have always loved about her because for some reason her pleas were always heard.

'Mum can we go to the fair?'

The adults of the house knew it was what we'd all been waiting for as soon as Ian and Sue had walked through the door.

'Mum, *can we*?'

Mum nodded, Kelly jumped for joy and I got my coat all in the space of ten seconds, it happened *so* quick that nobody had time to catch their breath. Then in the middle of all the merriment Sue pulled a face. Not a nice face, but an expression you'd show if you were unhappy about something.

'Hold on everyone.'

Sue looked at my Mother.

'You *will* remember to hold her hand *won't* you Sylvie?'

'Of course I will.'

My Mother replied, unsure of the motivation behind the question.

'Don't let her out of your sight either.'

'I won't.'

'Cause you know what these kids are like, they see something and they're off like a shot.'

What was this woman going on about? I mean, my Mother had two children of her own she knew what looking after spoilt children involved, she was hardly an amateur. Sue smiled.

'If you have any problems just give us a call here and Ian will pick you up in the car.'

My Mother bit her lip and exited the house with three extremely eager children in tow. Sue comments were nowhere near as acidic as the comments she had heard as a child, but she could never remember feeling more hurt in her life. The *one* role she cherished, the single thing that she thought she was damn good at, had been put into question by someone she considered a close friend. First she cursed her under her breath and then later when Ian and Sue had gone home she wept like a baby. Was she always going to be made to feel inadequate, even in the safety of her own home? Remembering seeing my Mother cry like that still brings a lump to my throat today, but thankfully it was the turning point in her condition. She never realised that her personal experiences would mar people's perception of her as a Mother, and she would change that even if it meant changing the very fabric of her personality.

Everyone in the family was aware of My Mother's eating disorder, after all it's not the easiest thing in the world to disguise, but they never knew of its intensity. If they did, they would never had of joked about it in the way that they did over the years, because all those jokes stopped my Mother's healing inside.

When I look to my Mothers past I'm sometimes tempted to get angry, I start wishing all sorts of things but I know this won't help, so I now tend to celebrate her ways and her past life as a monument to survival. After everything my Mother went through as a child she still got through it, and her healing acts as an inspiration to all the people who've ever lost faith in the world, because today she lives life as a different person. The scars of her past will always be there and she knows that, but never again will the memory of her family be able to touch her. For she's got her little house now, a husband who loves her, and two adoring children, and no ghost can take that away.

CHAPTER 5
Shadow

Drawing me in,
You took my child away.
Smashed it to pieces with exactness,
And spite.
Kissed me with prospect,
Only to take the sunlight away.
I blame *you* moonfaced child.
You, my mirror reflection, my shadow self,
And heart.

I'm standing in a pub called, 'The Forest' in a Welsh valley town called Trefforest, that's three F's in case anyone hasn't noticed. Outside it's pissing down but inside there's a party going on, there always is somewhere in Wales. The music on the jukebox is recognisable, but not to me, something being played at this volume is *never* recognisable to me, but the beer is good and I'll soon go onto tea and biscuits as closing time is looming up.

As I angle for a last drink at the bar I wave my yellow student union card which guarantees me a pint for one pound fifty and I think. My change of lifestyle has been a culture shock, a great big slap in the face, and it doesn't matter how many pairs of young firm breasts I see I still feel troubled. You see, it was as if the whole world had moved on in my marital absence and changed the social rules to everything. To normal folk something like this is usually refreshing, what is it they say? *'A change is as good as a rest'*. Don't believe them, it's crap, change means learning, learning means hard work. It's not all negative though, I *have* learnt things, the fact that I never wished to know those things is neither here nor there.

For instance, femininity is gone, dead in the grass. Women now fart and burp with the best of them, and that's just the tip of the iceberg. The art of polite conversation is also extinct and this saddens me, because I love small talk, it helps me to live in a constant state of denial which I've always found extremely comforting. I mean, why live in reality when a perfectly good state of fantasy will keep the doldrums away? I've tried sharing these thoughts but I'm told that those days are gone now, as unfashionable as my mullet and flares. Now I have to face people with warmth and honesty, phone calls from friends asking me soul searching questions designed to put me in touch with my real self. It's crazy, I should love this kind of thing but I don't because I realise that I'm an outsider. Not because of my age, but because of my ageing mindset. I know I don't fit, I really don't but that's okay because I'm not depressed or anything. I just wish I could enjoy the loose boundaries of 'student-dom' more instead of applying thirty something rules to everything. I wish I could enjoy the artistic freedom that learning brings and all the intrinsic rewards but I can't. I feel sad, and I feel guilty.

All this is extremely unnerving because when you get to the ripe old age of twenty-nine you like to think that nothing can shock you anymore. You like to think that your life experience has adequately equipped you for any situation out of the norm. Then you get hit by a thunderbolt, something like a divorce, and then you realise what naïve sap you really are.

My First Gambling Crime

A big family, plenty of working class money, it doesn't take a genius to figure out that 'ing' and 'ism' were two words strongly attached to the Flynn ideology, and being part of this collective I guessed it wouldn't be too long before I was exposed to the seedy 'Flynn' world of winning and loosing. I was never that attracted to cards and I always thought that turf accountants were too close to lawyers, so I never really ventured into a 'bookies'. This alone I thought would be enough to protect me from my family's way of life, but every Caesar has his Brutus and naivete was to be my downfall. You see, not all gambling takes place at the card table or betting shop, and I believe that the will to gamble was as intrinsic as the 'Flynn' will to breathe, so being caught was just a matter of time.

Up until the third year at secondary school I loved PE then Mr. Dean with his ginger mop of hair took over. That carrot topped nazi took the fun out of everything from rounders to cross-country. Rather than let us just play he had to draw these bloody diagrams on chalkboards, stuff about strategies and leadership, we didn't want that. When we did get the opportunity to kick a ball around it was always under the careful tutelage of Mr. Dean and his amazing whistle. A harsh tackle, a questionable off side and bad language would all receive a blow of his whistle followed by a fifteen-minute lecture. All that stopping and starting was awful and by the fourth week of term everybody had just about had enough, but *nobody* had the gumption to do anything about it. The others may have been weak but I wasn't going to stand for it, I wasn't about to let this *mere* teacher blaspheme the sports halls with chalkboards and rules. So, after much discussion in the playground me and two others decided to engage in a silent protest by leaving our sports kits at home and peacefully abstaining from any lessons taken by the evil Mr. Dean. That would show him wouldn't it? Surely after seeing his three star pupils forget their kit week after week he would question his teaching techniques.

When we forgot our sports kit for the third week running Mr. Dean guessed that there was a mutiny afoot, and being a democratic man who didn't take anything personally, punished us. No longer were we able to sit quietly in the corner of the sports hall and watch all the idiots run round chasing a ball. That luxury was cancelled as soon as our protest reached twenty-one days. On day twenty-two we were relegated to fetching his whistle and cleaning his office, there's nothing like being a successful revolutionary. Bastard. This show of power did nothing to dishearten our spirits though, because we arrogantly saw ourselves as the customers. All right, British people were not the type of people to usually complain, but that didn't give the ruling classes the right to provide a shoddy service to us customers.

As the weeks passed the dissent grew, Mr. Dean couldn't even look us in the eyes as he handed out our 'skivy' duties. Unable to be pleasant in the climate of protest he would just look at his feet and say,

'Clean this.'

Or.

'Empty that.'

We may have felt empowered but in reality Mr. Dean was *still* the individual with all the aces in his hand, so we hatched a plan. A dirty great plan with winners, losers, gambling and crime.

For the first two years of my secondary education I went to a mixed catholic school in Dover called St. Edmund's. It was, and still is a great school and has a wonderful reputation for discipline. Like most catholic schools of the time it had a strict dress code that was to include a zero tolerance policy in regards to jewellery and fashionable clothing. Now I don't know how things were handled in other schools but at St. Edmund's if you were found to be wearing something that wasn't on the dress code it was confiscated. Locked away in the Sports master's office for safe keeping until the end of term, I don't know if they'd get away with that now. It didn't matter how expensive an illegal item was it was still taken, taken labelled and stored in brown sacks in the corner.

This wasn't the case with jewellery, rings and bracelets were too valuable to put in a sack so they were placed in jam jars and locked in the cupboard for safe keeping. Jar after bloody jar of them, all sitting in Mr. Dean's office. Of course this treasure throve of goodies was always a talking point when your luck was down but because of the nature of our pupils we were rarely extended the opportunity to get anywhere near the booty. Every class has a bullshiter, and I had been told many fantasy stories about the thousands that sat in that cupboard but it wasn't until I saw it myself that I was able to make a judgement. Looking at the inside of the cupboard I could see that some of the stuff was real tacky, gold and plastic crap with letters engraved across the front, they wouldn't have even made the Argos catalogue. However, in the jars on the higher shelves the rings tended to be slightly more expensive. I had seen some of these rings before, these were those dummy engagement rings given to third year girls by older boys looking for a quick leg across. 'Fumbling rings' we used call them and estimating the possible value of that cupboard I came to the conclusion that St. Edmund's RC had the biggest collection of virgin girls in the world. I didn't need proof to come to that conclusion, here was the *proof* sitting right in front of me: a chest of random gold! I hated Mr. Dean, I hated my cleaning job, but I did have a key to that cupboard, worse still, I had a handful of sticky fingers too.

The games register was taken at nine on the dot Monday morning. When your name was called you either answered 'present' or 'no kit'. At the end of the register those with kit were instructed to change, and those without had to form a queue to give their excuses to Mr. Dean. People with sick notes or low absence rates were given clement duties like tidying the crash mats in the main hall, and that was alright for them. Serial offenders on the other hand like yours truly were given two keys one to the sport masters office and one to and cleaning cupboard, and then told to get on with it! For my plan to work we *all* had to be icy cool. One mistake and we wouldn't be able to sit down for a week let alone remain at the school as pupils.

Monday mornings starting at 9am Adrian would collect a bunch of keys along with an A4 piece of paper that contained our working duties for the period. While he was busy getting our mops and brooms from across the hallway we would enter the sport master's office, more importantly the *treasure* cupboard. Dave who was my right hand man would dart between the office and the hallway ready to create a diversion if anyone walked by. Whilst I had the more challenging duty of selecting fifteen inconspicuous rings from the jars on the shelves, ready for resale at the local second hand shop. We didn't take anything for the first couple of weeks because we wanted to see if the logistics of our plan was workable, thankfully it was. The real beauty though was the subtlety of our theft, firstly it was strictly a one off event, and secondly fifteen rings was all we'd take, no more, just enough to sort ourselves out. More than fifteen would spark interest from big brother with the ginger wig upstairs, and that was the last thing we wanted to happen.

To be labelled a thief is bad enough, but to be labelled a thief in a catholic school is as good as eternal damnation in the fiery wastes of hell. So fifteen was all we'd take.

This control worked well until our sweet and crisp oasis ran dry the succeeding morning, then we found ourselves justifying another possible heist. If they didn't miss fifteen rings then surely they wouldn't miss thirty. This greed was later to be fuelled by the fact that each time we sold them to the man at the second hand shop we'd get less and less money. Cunning bastard! *He knew* that this jewellery was acquired by ill-gotten means and felt it was his right to milk the situation for all it was worth. This was a good lesson learned, I may not have liked the power this snake held, but like or not his status was superior to mine in this environment. When it comes down to it, criminals are power*less*. There's no rules, no criminal's charter, it's pure capitalism, supply and demand. Something is only worth what someone is prepared to pay and a 'criminal's goods' are 'damaged goods' as far as the buyer is concerned. Yes I hated that little 'tight-arse' in the shop, but greed being the Achilles heal of *every* good criminal meant that we would revisit that place every week until we got caught.

Monday morning three weeks later after stealing the last ring we kind of knew that judgement day was looming. It was one of those logical sick feelings in your stomach that sort of chanted, 'you can't steal *all* the 'fumbling rings' without getting caught'. I tried to deny these voices in my head but everytime I thought I'd got rid of them they'd just come back louder and louder. I mean, what if some of these couples were still together at the end of term? Surely they'd want their rings back, surely the boys would want to reflect upon their investment. Now I was scared. The worst thing though, was that after all the risks we had taken, none of us had 'bean' to show for our labours. We hadn't invested anything, and nor had we spent our plunder on anything tangible. Instead we had wasted the whole bloody lot on nothing more than sweets crisps and chocolates, great criminals we were. I was just contemplating all these thoughts when the schools public address system sounded.

'Would Michael Flynn, David Parr and Adrian Petley please attend the Headmasters office immediately'.

Three names one location, I knew this spelt the end of our fledgling criminal careers, people in our school only ever got called to the Headmasters office for caning or expulsion. What the hell was I going to tell my parents?

'Gentlemen, do you know why you've been called here today?'

We all shook our heads.

'Think carefully now.' The Headmaster said.

'Is it because we haven't done our English homework Sir?'

Was David's pathetic opening gambit. The Headmaster frowned.

'No, I'm afraid it's nothing at all to do with homework, it's something much more serious.'

My heart sank and my mouth went dry, we really were up shit creek without a paddle this time.

'Is it because we keep forgetting our sports kit?' Was Adrian's reply, the Headmaster took a step forward closing the distance down between the four of us.

'You're getting warmer, *try again*?'

Adrian got worried, he knew he had already said too much.

'I don't know what you're talking about Sir.'

'Oh I think we both know that's a lie, don't you?'

This was getting scary now. Not only had he closed the space down between us he had also taken on this weird sort of persona. Any second now I was expecting him to shine a torchlight in our faces and say, 'we have ways of making you talk'.

'What about you *Flynn*, what do you have to say for yourself?'

There was a short stagnant silence, I choose my words carefully hoping that I could make a peace offering with some humble assertion.

'Sir, I am disappointed that you've had to take time out of your working day to deal with this situation.'

'And what situation would that be Flynn?'

Shit! What do I say now? I couldn't be the one to blurt the truth, that would be worse than getting the cane.

'Whatever situation we've been brought here for.'

He smiled, and took a step back.

'Gentlemen, *and I do use that term loosely*. I have summonsed you here to help me in a case of missing property.' He paused, and opened his desk draw.

'It would appear that certain items of jewellery have gone missing from Mr. Dean's office. Items of great worth. Do you three know anything about that?'

He was on to us, we stood still like statues. If we spoke, it would only have been to lie so silence was the preferable option. He could hit us for lying, but hitting us for being silent didn't sit well with his modern teaching philosophy.

'*Well?*'

He shouted taking his stick from out of the draw and banging it on the desk. Adrian whimpered.

'What is it Petley, you got something to say?'

A tear ran down Adrian's cheek.

If you have, say it now, or I swear in the name of Jesus Christ I'll make you the sorriest pupil in this school.'

I figured the tide was against us. Whether we liked it or not we going to get the stick, (lovingly known as 'uncle bend-over') so in my infinite wisdom I decided to take charge of the situation to get our power back.

Sir, I have something to say.'

The Headmaster swooped over, fangs dripping with blood.

'Yes Flynn, *what is it?*'

'Sir, we took the jewellery.'

The other two stared at me in disbelief, I'd told the truth! I had done the *one thing* that had nobody expected, I had owned up to my crimes. The Headmaster's demeanour immediately changed.

'That's very brave of you Flynn, that took guts. Well done!'

It wasn't brave at all, it was strategic. I knew we were done for as soon as we were called to the office, so I figured that if I owned up first, my punishment wouldn't be so severe.

Yes it was mercenary but there again I'd always felt I'd had a low pain threshold, so why should I suffer when the others could take more of the discomfort.

The Headmaster travelled to his filing cabinet and pulled out a handful of forms, without raising his head from the desk he wrote all of our names and addresses down.

'Of course all of your parents will have to be notified, I say this because they're obvious compensation claims to consider for which I doubt you have funds to pay.'

He paused. 'I won't call the Police, but that doesn't admonish you from punishment boys.'

Well, at least we weren't being expelled. Expulsion was a horrible thing to explain to two parents who had a love of corporal punishment, so whatever cards were dealt after this point would be seen as a bonus by me. He sighed and looked up from his forms.

'I don't enjoy this side of my work, I don't suppose any God fearing man would. I know you've admitted to your actions and that is noble in itself. However, I *have* to be sure that you've all repented. *I have to be sure* that you're all truly sorry for your crimes against this school and against God.'

David prematurely piped up, eager to save his hide.

'Sir, we're all really sorry. You wouldn't believe the guilt we've felt over this, only the other day we were saying we'd have to own up and....'

'Shut up! I didn't ask for your opinion.'

Great! We'd pissed him off again. Good old David, just when we'd achieved a karma of 'honesty' he had to go and ruin it by lying. Why couldn't he have just kept his gob shut and let this sadistic little nobody prattle on about the ten commandments and the last temptation of Christ. At least he'd be relaxed when he whacked us with the stick, at least he'd being thinking warm thoughts of us as he made our palms numb, now he'd be thinking all manner of things.

He picked up his stick and walked over to the three of us who were standing in an impromptu line.

'David, why did you take the rings?'

David swallowed, the very words made the hairs on the back of his neck stand up. In the short span of his life he had never been asked a question so directly.

'For money Sir.'

'And what did you spend this money on?'

'Sweets and Crisps Sir.'

'Hold out your hands.'

The Headmaster drew his 'stick-hand' up high and brought it down with such strength that the air around it whooshed through the room. Six times on each hand he hit him, each time David whimpered. He was such a tough kid because I'd known kids to pass out after the first strike, not him though. He wouldn't have given the bastard the pleasure of .even seeing him cry, on the final strike he even managed to smile at him. Pity the same couldn't have been said for poor old Adrian. He was sporting a rather wet leg and a possible smelly lump in the back of his trousers.

'Adrian, why did you take the rings?'

Adrian's time had just ran out, so the stupid git just repeated David's excuses for the crimes. For some reason this really annoyed the pervert with the cane in his hand for he stuck Adrian with what seemed like *more* force. Adrian cried his eyes out and begged for mercy but on and on the cane hit him, on the hands and on the back. I had to think quick because things were not looking good for me, he had warmed himself up on David and was now really cooking on poor old Adrian. What would happen by the time he really found his pace and got to me?

'Michael, why did you steal the rings?'

The other two looked at me, they knew I was planning something.

'To fuel an addiction Sir.'

The Headmaster took a surprised step back, he been expecting to hear the same answers and was now confused.

'A what?'

'An addiction Sir, I've been trying to fight for some time now.'

He frowned unsure of how to continue.

'What type of addiction?'

'The worst kind Sir.'

I said this for dramatic effect feeling that it might buy me a little more time.

'Which is?'

'Gambling Sir.'

I could almost feel him breathe a sigh of relief. The last thing he wanted was the schools name slapped across the local papers saying something like, 'St. Edmund's junkie pupils'.

'Have you tried to get help for this problem?'

'I've prayed for help, but as of yet I've been too ashamed to seek formal assistance Sir.'

He lowered his cane, and I continued my verbal escape.

'I didn't know what to do Sir, I didn't want to do these horrible things but some sort of evil impulse took over.'

'And what did you spend your money on?'

I couldn't say betting shops, he knew I'd never be able to lay a bet down in my school uniform. So I picked the next best thing that all teenage boys have access to.

'Fruit machines Sir.'

'Fruit machines? Do you mean one arm bandits?'

Of course I meant one-arm bandits, what century did he live in?

'Yes Sir.'

The other two looked horrified, what was I doing? They had already been beaten once this morning and my lies were placing them in the way of another possible thump. It was important that I tread carefully from this point on, stretch the truth too much and I'd blow it.

'And how long have you had this condition?'
The Headmaster questioned.
'Since puberty Sir.'

The other two sniggered, 'puberty' was still a risky word to say to a Headmaster then, but a credible word to use in a situation like this. 'Puberty' suggested medical investigation, it gave a clinical edge to my problem diffusing my greed. After all I couldn't help myself, *I was an addict*.

'And at what age did your puberty start?'
'Thirteen Sir.'

I knew that when we left that office the other two would take great joy in disclosing that information to the whole school. Adrian and David sniggered again.

'You two got something to say?'
The words 'No Sir' echoed round the office.
'Well then, you're dismissed. Return to your classes.'

This was looking good, not only had I avoided the stick thus far, I also had the old git feeling sorry for me. The only concern now was keeping a straight face, what would I do if he asked me something like, '*Do you wet the bed?*'

Adrian and David left the office scowling, I don't think they appreciated the fact that I had saved *my* skin and not theirs. As it stood I would have to work hard in here, but I would also have to work hard outside to avoid another beating at the hands of my jealous friends. Why are teenage boys like that?

The Headmaster shut the door behind them and drew his breath, his tight angry frame had now relaxed a little.

'It is a terrible thing you have told me here today, but I still cannot condone your actions, I don't think that would be ethical. However, if you are *truly* in a state of need, then I cannot punish you for something you are not in control of. What I'm saying is, that if you need help, I will get it for you. How do you feel about that Flynn?'

I smiled, not a big toothy grin but a humble smile of thanks. I may have wanted to jump for joy but I wasn't going to, it was still important that I carried off my 'victim-like persona'. Business was almost concluded, all I needed now was a *good final line* so I could complete my escape.

'Thank-you very much Sir, it's more than anyone else has done for me.'

The Headmaster nodded feeling he had done the right thing, this act of kindness would surely put him on the road to heaven.

'You'll be pleased to know that I'm sparing you corporal punishment on the grounds of your honesty Flynn, but *I do* expect you to follow my help, is that clear?'

I nodded, yes I had escaped 'corporal punishment' as he put it, but I didn't like the sound of 'help'. It raised another situation in which I would have to lie again. The Headmaster continued.

'In instances like this we like to take a modern approach and accept that not everything can be solved by prayer. Some challenges need the help of a specialist, do you know what a specialist is Flynn?'

I didn't like the word 'specialist' either. 'Specialist' was too close to expert something that he wasn't.

'What I'm going to suggest is not the nicest of expeditions, but It's important to remember that the path with the most obstacles often provides the richest journey. Obviously I will discuss this with your parents, but I would like you to see the school psychologist. What do you think of that?'

Now, I *really* was in the crap. 'What did I think?' I thought I was up shit creek without a paddle is what I thought. Those 'head doctors' were trained for seven years at universities across the country and could spot a liar like me a mile off. I should have just accepted the beating that was coming to me and left like the others, but oh no, I had to get all clever and dig myself a deeper hole.

'Thank-you very much Sir, but do you think it's necessary. I mean, with the schools budget being tight and everything?'

'Nonsense! You'll get the help you need. Now go back to class, your parents will contacted in due course.'

That was it sentence had been passed, and as I left the office I remember thinking that things had just got a whole lot more complicated, how was I going to explain this to my parents? Reasonable they were, stupid they were not. I remember doing a lot of worrying that day because 'difficult' didn't begin to express the hole that I had now dug for myself. Convincing them that from leaving the house that morning to returning in the afternoon I had picked up an addiction was no meant feat. Fortunately by the time I got home most of the groundwork had be done by the headmaster who had proactively warned my parents of my crimes and the solutions that would follow them. This simple action really 'bolloxed' my plan by taking away the element of surprise, and allowing my parents to prepare a water tight prosecution case upon my return.

'Sit down, we want to talk to you.' As soon as I got through the door.

'Can I go to my room first?'

'No, we want to talk to you now.'

There was no malice in their voices, their anger had moved forward from that and now stood somewhere round *concern*, but I still felt I needed time.

'Can I at least use the toilet?'

They shook their heads and pointed to a chair in the front living room where they wanted me to sit and talk.

My Father just listened saying nothing, he wasn't sold on my plight but *was* interested in where my tale was going. My Mother on the other hand was in tears at my make believe disablement, saying over and over that she had failed as a parent, this wasn't so good. I hated seeing my Mother cry, there had been too many tears in her life already and the thought of me causing her some more ripped me apart.

'You'll have to get help.' My Mother whimpered.

'It was only a few rings Mum.'

Ninety to be precise, but I didn't think it was a good idea to mention that. It was also a good idea *not* to mention the fact that my Mother's upset was the only saving grace between me and a good hiding from my Dad. Mercenary again, but as long as she was crying he wouldn't raise a hand to me in fear of bringing the past back to her.

'It doesn't matter if you steal once or a hundred times, a thief is a thief!'

'I couldn't help myself.'

'It looks like you helped yourself pretty well to me.'

This was exactly the type of logic I didn't need, already my Mother was drying her eyes.

'I didn't have any money.'

'Then you should have got a Saturday job, you didn't have to do this.'

Shit! When did he become so clever? I had to recover this situation before it went totally 'tits up' and swallowed me whole.

'I wanted to buy you both decent Christmas presents.'

My Mother lowered her head in shame, what the hell was I doing? I should have stopped it right there and then but I couldn't. Everytime I found a pregnant pause to commence my confession, my Father would pipe up with some smart-ass question and place me on the defensive again.

'So what's going to happen now?'

'They've referred me to a specialist.'

Mum sobbed, Dad laughed.

'What type of specialist?'

'One that specialises in my type of problem.'

'What lying?'

Mum momentarily stopped crying and looked me in the eyes, up until this point she hadn't even considered the possibility of perjury, and never would have if it wasn't for my Father. A second's silence ran through the room, a sort of Mexican stand-off if you will. Then, from the depths of her sorrow my Mother found the strength to ask the one question that was now on her mind.

'You're not lying are you Mick?'

I was done for again! Why couldn't I have had the slow parents that my friends had? Why the hell did I have to have Sherlock Holmes and Dr. Watson as a Mother and Father?

'Well?'

My Father beckoned. This directness was bad for the situation because it placed me in a dead end alley with limited options. I took a deep breath. Whether I liked it or not, a gauntlet had been thrown down, and I had to either confront this challenge or retreat from it. To remain motionless at this moment would mean defeat, something I wasn't very good at.

'That's the problem with you two, you never pay any attention to me and my problems, it's always you, you, you!'

I hit the coffee table with the palms of my hands to amplify my plight, all the time calculating my escape. I needed to get to some space between me and them before I had to do something drastic like tell the truth.

'Nobody understands me!'

I shouted whilst standing to my feet.

'I'm going to my room'.

'No you're not!'

My Father boomed back, it was always more scary when he shouted. We both looked at my Mother for support, although extremely quiet in confrontational environments her casting vote was all important here, but from the look of it my Mother was still undecided about the whole thing. She just sat there with a blank expression on her face, I've heard that social workers refer to this as, 'dynamic non-intervention'. (Sounds about right doesn't it?)

'Tell him Sylvie, tell him he has to sit down and answer my questions'.

Mum was biting her lip and sucking her teeth, something she always done during times of stress. Little did we know that many years later Anthony Hopkins would steal this technique and successfully incorporate it into the character of Hannibal Lector.

Mum looked at me. She knew I was guilty but didn't have the heart to administer a lecture so she said,

'Let him go to his room'.

"What?"

My Father complained but it was useless, he could throw a tantrum if he wanted but it still wouldn't change my Mother's decision, she had spoken. I left the room with a bowed head unable to make eye contact with the two people I called parents, this was not a nice situation to be in. Then it struck me really hard, if I had failed to convince my parents, how the hell was I going to convince the school psychologist who specialised in these types of problems?

In my room that night I mulled over the days events and wondered again how I had got myself into this mess, what had started off as a collusion between the three of us was now a public affair. In two days I would be called to the visitors office and have all my insecurities dragged out in front of a guy I had never met before. This was stressful enough but knowing that I also had to convince him of my make believe condition didn't make me feel any easier. Sitting my room I could have kicked myself that night, because my innate fear of pain had placed me in this predicament and now it was up to my intelligence to get me out of it! Surely it couldn't be that difficult though? I mean, I had watched *all* the chat shows under the sun for a decade or more so I felt I had a good understanding of what constituted anti-social behaviour. It was now just a case of getting the flavour of those things together and amplifying them with words and actions, but how do you project insanity? Dribbling was definitely out, too cliché. Violence would be no use to me either, knowing my luck I'd probably be roughed up and stuck in a straight jacket or something. No, I had to be Jack Nicolson in 'one flew over the cuckoo's nest', I had to be Brando in 'street car', I had to be Michael Flynn faking a fetish. I racked my brains for weird bizarre things to say to the head doctor but when I finally met him, the best I could come up with was,

'I like the way the money comes out.'

'What do you mean?' Said Freud on the armchair with his clipboard, God I was fucked.

'I like the sound it makes as the coins hit the pan.'

'Tell me more about that.'

What more was there to say than what I had already said?

'What do you mean?'

'You said you liked the sound of the money hitting the pan, why do you like that sound? What kind of feelings does it evoke when a boy like you hits jackpot? That's what I'm trying to get at.'

'Oh'.I said, still oblivious to where this session was going.

'Well, as I said when the money hits the pan I like it, I like it because I'm rich.'

'Why, do you consider yourself poor then?'

How many questions was this bastard going to ask? I put ten pence in, I push the start button, three cherries come up and I win a pound, it makes me happy. Simple, what more is there than that?

'No not poor.'

'Then why did you use the word rich?'

I didn't know why I used the word rich, just like I didn't know how the lies were going to come out, he asked a question and I gave him an answer. If I knew why I gave that answer I'd probably be sitting in his chair.

'I don't know why I used that word, I guess I just want more all the time.'

'Is that so?'

'Yes, sometimes.'

He lowered his head and scribbled something on the pad of paper. I could see he wasn't satisfied with that answer, because something as vague as 'wanting more' couldn't be pigeon-holed into a category in one of his fancy books. I didn't let this bother me though because as far as I was concerned 'wanting more' was a human occupation that engulfed us all from time to time and who was he to judge that?

'But how much more is how much more?'

'I'm sorry.'

'How much more is how much more?'

How was I supposed to answer that? Did I tell him that too much was never enough and really fox him, or did I just come clean and tell him that I would be happy with a ten percent increase on my pocket money allowance. This was mad. Every lie I told led to another lie, and with each lie I became more unconfident.

'I'm sorry I don't understand.'

The head doctor huffed, blessed with patience he wasn't.

'I'm trying to establish how deep your desire runs Michael, do you envisage yourself reaching a level of wealth where you would be content, or do you think you'll always be the type of person who want's more?' Laying on that leather couch I knew it didn't matter because either way I was buggered. He wasn't convinced with my little tale of woe, he hadn't once nodded *or* smiled all the way through my opening speech. Nor had he shown any empathy when I explained to him the terrible guilt I was experiencing everytime I passed a jewellers.

'I want more'. I announced.

'Much more. I want a paper round, a Saturday job, and more than that I want some savings in the bank.'

He scribbled frantically on his pad again.

'Does that answer your question?'

'Oh yes.'

He smiled.

'I think we'll wrap this up for today, you can return to your lessons. Thank-you for your time Michael.'

Great, he was finally being nice to me.

'Same time next week?' I inquired.

'No, that won't be necessary, I'll forward my report to the school and then onto your parents. They'll advice you of the next stage.'

That didn't sound good, I thought I'd get at least six or seven sessions out of this Victorian throwback, but no, one session and it's all over and done with. Was he referring me onto another specialist or was he signing my death warrant?

'I don't understand'

The head doctor grinned.

'Oh you will don't worry, run along now and you'll catch the last half hour of mathematics.'

He didn't need to say he didn't believe me, the bloody words were written all across his face, but what would become of me now? It would take a minor miracle to save my lying ass from the cane now, because as it stood things between me and the big fella upstairs were not that hot at the moment. I hadn't been to confession in twelve months and I had also dropped religious studies from my 'O' level curriculum. To pray now would make me as hypocritical as the Pharisees in the temple signing Christ's death warrant, and that was something I wasn't prepared to do. I needed to slow down and take control, things were moving way too fast.

Through my questionable actions I had exhausted plans A and B, and now desperately needed a plan C. The kind of plan which would provide amnesty from now until my last day of school. This was pure fantasy of course but it still didn't stop me hoping, the same way I couldn't stop hoping that Mr. Dean would just crawl back under a rock and return to the Neanderthal species he originated from.

After knocking politely I sat at the back of the math's class and took notes for the last half hour, usually I'd doodle but I thought in light of the situation I'd show a more adept side of my personality, but this wasn't to save me. This wasn't to save me because I stupidly thought that the informal forty-eight hours I had given myself for a plan C would be granted. The schools public address system sounded and everyone went quiet.

'Would Michael Flynn please attend the headmasters office immediately'

I gulped, it was the only thing I could do to stop myself from throwing up. The thought of finally coming face to face with uncle bend over was a frightening contemplation for a boy who had a pre-mentioned fear of pain. I sat at my desk frozen with fright. Everybody turned round and the lesson stopped, being summonsed to the Headmasters office twice in the space of ten days spelt trouble, and the crowds at the desks could smell it like vultures circling a dead man.

'Well'.

The math's teacher said.

"Shouldn't you be getting along?"

I nodded, and got my things together. This whole situation had run away with itself and on some level I was pleased that it would now all be over and done with in a few minutes, I was tired and I felt ill. I slung my bag over my shoulder with the girls whispering behind my back and left the classroom unafraid of what was to become of me. At the time getting one up on Mr. Dean was nice just like the money was nice too, but when I added it all up in my head I had to admit that it just wasn't worth it. For the thirty or so pounds that I had received I had made myself incredibly ill. The address system sounded again but his time in a more curt manor.

"Would Michael Flynn *please* attend the headmasters office immediately."

I picked up my pace and ran down the stairs but was met halfway up by the Headmaster who was sporting a terrible frown.

'You! Go to my office. I am summoning your parents, and then I'll meet you there myself. Do not touch anything, is that clear?'

'Yes Sir.'

I got to the office and walked inside, strangely I wasn't frightened anymore. I knew what was going to happen and I thought it best to take my punishment like a man, the same way David had. I'd let him say what he had to say, then I'd hold my hands out and let him strike me, I had nothing left anymore except my dignity. The Headmaster entered the office.

'Flynn, I've contacted your parents and they are unable to attend due to working commitments.'

He paused, I could tell he was excited at the thought of justice, this was a guy who got sexually aroused at the thought of corporal punishment. If he had his way he would've have handled all situations of confrontation in this way.

'Do I need to ask you why you think you've been brought here again?'

I wouldn't lie anymore this just made things worse, the last thing I wanted was another circuit of this merry go round. I wanted off and I wanted off now.

'No Sir, I know why I'm here. I'm here because I lied.'

It was so nice to say those words, so beautiful to finally release myself from the stress, just saying that sentence made me feel a hundred pounds lighter.

'Good.'

He smiled.

'Well, as I said I spoke to your parents. *And* in light of our findings I have decided to administer the same punishment to you as I gave to the others as well as suspending you from the school premises for seven days. How do you feel about that?'

'Relieved Sir.'

The Headmaster swallowed hard and took uncle bend over out from the draw of the desk.

'Hold your hands out.'

CHAPTER 6
Sister

I'm grieved we were never peerless companions.
Sorry, I never grasped your open hand.
Regretful I competed with you.
In cases of wasteful ceaseless bland.

"So Michael, what do you want to do when you finish your studies?"

What kind of question was that to ask? She was only my careers tutor at the University.

"I'm not totally sure you see, I'm kind of hoping that this degree will give me different options."

She stared hard at me.

"I'm not quite sure I understand what you mean."

"Well, before I came here I always worked in business, I was never qualified to do anything else, well, not anything else that paid a decent salary anyway." She tapped her pencil on her teeth.

"So you're hoping that this degree will offer you different paths?"

I nodded.

"And what are you studying again?"

"Psychology and drama."

She made one of those '*Hmmm*' sounds, I hate those sounds they give me a sweaty ass. Suddenly nothing is comfortable, you have to move.

"Are you okay there Michael?"

"Fine, you were saying about my degree choice."

She smiled a false smile and wet her lips.

"Hmmm,"

There was that noise again, I clenched the cheeks of my backside together in order to hamper movement on the squeaky leather chair.

"There's teaching I suppose, you ever thought about teaching?"

Doesn't every student when there's nothing else to do I thought.

"A bit."

"A *'bit'*! Sounds *'a bit'* vacant to me Michael."

Yeah, maybe it was, but she wasn't me. She didn't have the million and one things to contend with on a daily basis that I did. She didn't have to live in a house with three girls, she didn't have just five minutes in the bathroom every morning, and she probably didn't have the fear of failure that I had either. It was alright for her sitting there, in her Laura Ashley jacket, free of worry on thirty thousand pounds a year, I mean how much stress is there in a nine to four job? As far as I was concerned she could sit there as smug as she wanted and make all the adverse comments under the sun, I'd heard them all before anyway. What counted is that I knew where I was at that moment in time. Yes, I may not have had a clear idea of where I was going, but when I finished this degree I would have options, even teaching. None of that really mattered at this moment because this was a different battle. Was I going to let this jumped up academic keep me in child mode or was I going to strike back and take control?

"I do understand your concern, however when it comes to *my* future, I think it's up to me how long I take over it."

Fifteen love Michael Flynn.

"Well, how long have you got Michael?"
Fifteen all.
"I don't think you're listening to me, as long as I want."
Thirty fifteen.
"Then what was the point of you attending this session today?"
Thirty all.
"Well, an understanding ear would have been nice."
Forty thirty.
"I think we'll conclude for today, don't you?"
Match postponed due to bad weather.

My Sister's Love Life

Sex is always a dodgy subject around your parents. As level headed as they may want to be in their attitudes and opinions they can never quite manage it. This isn't because they don't want to be modern parents or anything, it's because they can't getaway from the fact that someone else is shagging their child. Logic and fair play are leapfrogged further when they remember that they were doing exactly the same thing when they were your age, but it still doesn't make it any easier. *No one should be shagging their children, even if they are above the legal age of consent!* The flipside to this reality is denial, the misplaced belief that their children will remain virgins until the day that they marry. My Sister and I were lucky we had a set of modern parents so our sexual options were not diminished to knee trembling in dark alleyways, if our boyfriends or girlfriends wanted to stay over it was never a problem, until one night.

Poor Penny has always been unfortunate in love. *This is not her fault!* Because over the years she has dated a host of men from different socio-economic backgrounds and all of them have turned out to be 'total shits'. Speaking as her brother there was no bigger 'shit' than Simon Bourne. (Often named *'Still-Bourne'* by his work colleagues in light of his questionable cognitive processes) Well, you know when you get to that stage in life where you think you've seen everything, Simon sort of shattered that illusion for me. You see, there you are sailing along on the oceans of life, comfortable in your sexuality, and worldly wise in the rules of fair play. Then you meet someone like Simon Bourne and realise that there is always one more imbecile than you counted on. Simon was not only a total 'shit' he was also a policeman, in my books this would be termed as a 'double whammy of shit, with a blue tit'. I disliked him not because he was a policeman, and not because I was an overbearing Brother or anything. I had a problem with Simon because he made me embarrassed to be a man not because of the way he looked, but because of the way he acted. In the six months that they were together he must have used every trick in the book from coercion to emotional abuse to get what he wanted. He was definitely going to make a great Policeman as well as re-enforcing the belief that 'all men are bastards', and that's why I didn't like him.

Simon used to work shifts and this placed certain time management obstacles in the path of Penny who was still at that stage where she wanted to see him twenty-four hours a day. As I mentioned Penny and I were blessed with modern thinking parents, but I forgot to mention the fact that they were also proactive too. So, being the 'modern proactive' people that they were they decided that it was better to give Simon a front door key of his own, rather than deal with a frustrated undersexed daughter. That way when he was working shifts he could still rendezvous with Penny to 'bump uglies' at anytime of the night or day. Logical? Well it was until they broke up!

It was seven o'clock on a Saturday night just before his shift when Simon finally said the two words that Penny had been afraid to hear, 'It's over'. He'd said them in jest many times over the last six months, but this time he meant it and the walls of Penny's life came tumbling down like Jericco. She cried, quietly at first, then louder, and then louder again. At the time I wasn't too close to her but I couldn't help feeling sorry about the situation, nobody likes to see anyone cry and poor Penny was sobbing her heart out. As I combed my hair I could see her coast through a whole collection of insecurities from her reflection in the hallway mirror. 'What did I do wrong?' 'Why doesn't he love me?' It was *so* awful to see her like this. Even Mum and Dad broke their established code of silence and got involved

"Mick stop combing that effeminate mop of hair and speak to your Sister."

Effeminate! How could a Father say such a thing to a son? Just because he never grasped the idea of fashion doesn't mean I have to walk round like Forest Gump in BHS sweaters. I carried on preening, figuring it was the best way to ignore his comments.

"What do you want me to say exactly?

"You're her Brother, think of something."

My Mother chipped in. Great! She was full of suggestions. Why do parents always lay these guilt trips on you when you're just about to head out to the pub to meet some friends? *I didn't know what to bloody say to her.* What does a sarcastic Brother tell his baby Sister apart from, 'I told you so?'. I knew she didn't want to hear that so plummeted for something safer, something that sounded almost sincere.

"Penny I'm really sorry."

She looked at me and then cried some more.

"Couldn't you have thought of anything better to say?"

My Mother hissed at me. Sure I could have, I could have thought of lots of things. I could have said, 'never trust Satan in a blue suit.' or, 'all coppers are wankers' but I don't think she would have appreciated it. I ushered Mum into the kitchen.

"Look Mum, I'm really sorry Penny's upset. I really am, but nothing I say is going to make her feel any better, so I think it's best I just make myself scarce, you know, give the girl some space of her own."

My Mother stretched a look of false disappointment across her face.

"*So you're going to the pub*, is that what you're telling me?"

She knew me too well, so I stood there motionless afraid of digging a deeper hole by convincing her that I was going to church or something.

"Go on then, off you go. We'll look after your Sister. We'll look after you're Sister while you go out and celebrate."

Believe it or not my Mother wasn't Jewish but her words did twist like a knife through my heart. Of course I cared that Penny was upset, but there was nothing I could physically do. Yes I could hit Simon for all the 'shit' he'd put her through but that still wouldn't make him care for her anymore. So what more could I do than say to her again.

"Penny I'm *really* sorry."

This time she wailed louder, much louder and I thought it best that I leave via the backdoor on my way out. I don't know why I bothered I thought, even when I was being sincere it wasn't good enough. Maybe I should amplify my emotions by mourning for three days or something because I'm sure things were getting more unreasonable by the second in that house. I mean, I couldn't even comb my hair without being called a poof.

Back inside the house poor old Penny cried like a baby, this was *very* real and worried my parents. I suppose you kind of know that things are serious when someone starts heaving after running out of tears, and in my books that *bastard* policeman was responsible. Penny's upset affected everyone especially my Father who was suffering with breathing problems at the time, and my Mother too who was supposed to be working a night shift at an old people's home. After a brief conversation my parents endeavoured to establish calm by reorganising the sleeping arrangements of the house. They weren't experts in the topic of teenage romance because they'd been together since the age of thirteen, but they did have logical heads on their shoulders, and this logic told them that something had to be done. So for that night and that night only Dad would sleep in

Penny's room with the window open to ease his asthma, and Penny would sleep in my parents room with my Mother for comfort. Bless my parents for their simplicity because this way they would know that everyone was okay. As I tucked into my second pint of the evening the three of them were neatly tucked up in bed safe in the knowledge that Still-Bourne was gone and not coming back, that was just the beginning of their problems. Experience should have told them that an idiot like that would never know when to call it a day.

It's 1am and my thirty pounds is gone, nothing to show for it apart from a donner kebab stain on my white shirt, and a mouth like Gandhi's flip flop. I checked the ripped lining of my coat for hidden money, but finally accept that I'm penniless until next Friday. Having no money and a six mile walk home is an incredibly sobering experience at 1 am in the morning, but there was nothing I could do about it. So, I stuck my thumb out, put a false limp on, and headed off to my rightful place. Home. I'm not a con man but let me tell you, limping and hitching is an excellent technique for the weary nomad, especially if couples drive by. You see, unless they're married a man will always be eager to impress a woman, because women can never hate a kind man. Kind men always get *gold* at the end of the night. So what better way to express an act of kindness then to pick a limping hitch-hiker in the early hours of the morning? And that's what happened, fifteen minutes into my hike and I was picked up by a good Samaritan in a VW Beetle.

"Where are you going mate?" Said the Dutch looking man behind the wheel.

"Coxheath."

"What happened to your leg?" Asked his pretty blonde girlfriend.

"Oh, that's just a disablement I've had since I was a child."

It was an awful thing to say but how many people have morals at the age of nineteen? She winced and looked at her boyfriend who was obviously still eager to score some more kindness points for his night of passion. "Well look, it's not far out of our way, let us drop you to your door."

I felt guilty.

"You don't need to do that, I mean, don't go out of your way or anything."

The Dutch looking man glanced over at his girlfriend with a glint in his eyes and then he looked at me.

"Relax man, Coxheath's only five minutes out of our way, now come on, get in."

His blonde girlfriend slid into the back, she was proud of her kind Dutch looking fella.

I got in, and the VW Beetle shot off at speed.

"I'm Karel this is Sally, stick of gum?"

He held out a Wrigley's

"No thank-you."

He dropped down a gear and sped into a corner, my anal passage nearly collapsed.

"What's your name friend?"

"Michael." I stuttered.

"Would you like a beer? We have an icebox in the back if you're thirsty Michael."

"No thank-you, that's very kind of you though."

Karel changed back up into fourth gear gaining maximum speed on a straight known as Stone Street, I was frightened to ask him what he did in case he told me racing driver or something.

"I like your hair Michael." Said Sally from the back.

"Thanks very much, I wished my Father did."

This comment seemed to interest her.

"Why doesn't he like it?"

"He calls me a poof."

Karel laughed a Viking laugh and placed his hand on my thigh.

"I wouldn't worry about that, in Holland everyone worries about their hair, bisexuals, they're everywhere aren't they Sally."

Sally leant forward and nodded with enthusiasm.

"*It's true*, even the politicians are."

As if that would shock me.

"So what do you do for a living Karel?"

"Me?" He said taking his hand from my thigh and slamming the car into another bend.

"I'm a rave DJ, and Sally here's a dancer."

Great, locked in a *speeding* car with a *speed* freak. What would the headlines read tomorrow? '*Limping twat looses life*'

"What do you do for a living Mike?"

"I work for a supermarket chain as a trainee manager"

Karel took his eyes off of the road for a second.

"That's great Mike, feed the world, good karma man."

Good karma that was a joke, if I got home in one piece that would be good karma, if he travelled below one hundred miles an hour that would be good karma too.

"Thank-you Karel, but could you keep your eyes on the road."

Karel laughed.

"Relax man, I'm enchanted."

Great.

Back at the house my Father retired to my Sisters room with the window open for a good nights sleep. My Sister on the other hand was still upset by the evening's activities and retired with my Mother into her bedroom, everything was peaceful again in the Flynn household. Twenty minutes passed and everyone was sound asleep. Dad snored, Penny whimpered, and my Mother remained catatonic as she always did when she was asleep. The great thing about living in a place like Coxheath was the quiet, when you wanted to get away from everything it really was as simple as closing your door, but this silence was about to be broken.

Just after one thirty a car slowly pulled into the close waking no one. The car door opened a man got out, his footsteps crept up the drive to our house. This man was not a burglar, rapist or jewel thief, he was a policeman. He had come to make up with his girlfriend who he had upset earlier by saying he had never wanted to see her again. Yes, that's right *'Still-Bourne'* had done the one thing he had promised not to do, he had returned to play with my Sister's mind a little more. Why shouldn't he?

He still had a front door key, so strictly speaking this action could not be seen as breaking and entering. *'Still-Bourne'* placed the key in the door and opened it slowly, he had seen this done on Starsky and Hutch in the seventies and knew that, *'the word on the streets was to play it cool'*. This guy wasn't silly, he couldn't be, I mean after all he was a member of the armed Police squad and we all know how rational those guys are.

He closed the front door behind him, careful to not make any noise. Things like this made his heart beat fast, but he wasn't scared he knew Penny had a forgiving heart. She must have, after all the things he had done to destroy her confidence she still felt affection for him. Up the stairs he trod one by one until he reached my Sisters bedroom.

Karel and his amazing Beetle speed into Coxheath, screeching to a halt at the top of my road. The passenger door swung open and I was thrown out, the nice Dutch man of ten minutes before was gone.

"Fuck you man, I was only trying to be friendly you've given the whole evening bad vibes now."

The car door closed and off they sped again into the sunset, eager to find another drop out or sexual deviant. I dusted myself off and started the hundred yard walk to my house.

Inside the house *'Still Bourne'* could be seen standing outside the bedroom door, he was contemplating how he was going to handle his intended reconciliation with Penny. On the other side of the door lay my Father curled up tightly underneath the duvet. *'Still Bourne'* opened the door and crept into the bedroom slipping off his clothes as he did so, waking

Penny up at this stage would spoil the surprise of his apology. At about the same time the Policeman slipped his naked carcass next to my Fathers, I walked in downstairs.

"I'm really sorry about earlier, why don't we give it another go?"

My Father woke up unsure if he was dreaming or not.

"Come on Penny, let's just make love."

From downstairs I heard a scream. In a flash my Mother was up and all the lights were on. I ran up the stairs armed with a bread knife and met her on the landing, without a word of communication we burst into Penny's room eager to find the source of the scream. As the door opened we were faced with two naked men fighting in bed. Penny walked in.

"Simon, how could you? You promised me you'd never cheat again."

My Dad struggled to get up, but fell out of bed.

"Penny, it's not what you think."

Mum smiled, and I laughed, it appeared there was more than one poof in the household.

CHAPTER 7
Fame

The thrash that steams through the ensemble,
As villainous as the flash bulbs, as fake as the love.
Where do you people go?
The gold nugget headlines that tell of legends,
Men and women different to us.
Hounded and chased for thirty pieces of silver,
Kissed on the cheek, ears severed, denied.
Starlets, actors, musicians and 'it' girls,
Have you surrendered to realise the cost?
The riches in 'anonymous', the indulgence of disappearance.
Just stop to add it all up.

Do you know that the most stressful thing in my life at the moment is knowing that I don't have a home of my own. Forget Paul Young and all that rubbish about, *'Wherever I lay my hat is my home'* that's for teenagers. I'm thirty in three weeks time, the big three zero and I'm more unsettled now than I ever have been. People tell me not to worry and that when I finish my degree I'll be able to get a good job and a little place of my own. Fine, maybe that's true but that doesn't help me now. I want solitude, I want clean surfaces, I want a dog and I want to be able to eat bacon sandwiches without offending the other three vegetarians that I share my accommodation with. So don't tell me to relax and look to the future because the way I see it, I've got another three years of this bollocks and nobody seems to give a damn except me.

I don't want to be a hermit or a recluse I just want the decision. The opportunity to express myself in dead silence, the choice to watch what I want on television, and to read without the sound of Boyzone rattling through the walls. If it sounds like I'm moaning then I'm sorry, but I dare not say these things aloud in this house. Young girls and their music can be extremely treacherous things to walk around, to disrespect Ronan and the boys would be nothing short of Blasphemy. Believe me to say, 'turn that crap off' would be to seal my fate. So I've taken measures to help myself out, no I haven't plugged my ears, nor have I sound proofed my bedroom. Instead I've bought a houseboat, and on that boat I will find my peace and play my Bob Dylan albums as loud as I like. Not the most sensible thing to buy after a divorce, but I love the idea of being able to just up anchor and move to a new place if anyone pisses me off. Strange, but at the tender age of twenty-nine I have finally understood that an Englishman's home is his castle. I want to hide, I want to be anonymous, to be known or to be famous would be my worst nightmare come true at the moment.

The Talent Show

My parents absolutely adore the whole concept of fame, don't ask me why, they just do. So perverted is this desire that they will usually go to any length to secure an autograph from *anyone* who has been in the press for *anything*. I'm not knocking this because people have all manner of hobbies, and to me in my ignorant state even the concept of collecting stamps seems like a pathetic waste of time, but everyone's different. So here on paper let me say that the adoration of famous people makes me confused, but I don't think any less of anybody who queues up for hours on end to gain a scribble on a piece of paper. Sadly the only chance my parents ever had to be famous I ruined, and this story I hope stands as an apology for any heartache I may have caused them in taking their fifteen minutes away.

Ever since I can remember my parents have loved live entertainment, music dancing, comedy, anything. The smell of the greasepaint and the sound of people treading the boards are the tones and aromas that electrify my Mum and Dad. Secretly, I think my Dad would have loved to have been on the stage. A Max Miller type character who'd charm old ladies with safe jokes and quips about naughty milkmen and busty barmaids. My Mother on the other hand would have been a behind the scenes person, a set designer who would've created magnificent backdrops for the performers to ply their art on. Fate or bad luck I don't know which, but my parents were never granted the opportunity to free the muses that ran wild in their unconscious minds, but that never stopped them hoping.

This desire was to be granted one week at a talent show, after my Father full of bravado and red wine convinced the owner of the Warden Bay Hotel that he was a big name in the world of amateur boxing. Being a man who also loved fame he latched straight onto my Father who talked of pulling strings and guest appearances. This relationship developed and after two weeks of free vino and cucumber sandwiches they were both asked to be judges. Not just ordinary judges, but guest judges at the grand final on the 1st of December. This was just the kind of fame they coveted, a hundred hopefuls and their families all sitting in a room with them on the top table, for once they'd have all the power. These positions of responsibility were coercively perfect, a bath of applause and a shower of love, all in the space of four hours in this the holiest month of the calendar year. These two were in fame heaven.

My Father got on the telephone and told just about everyone, each time he told the story the size of venue would increase. What started as eight acts in a club from nowhere ended up as Saturday night at the Palladium, this thing was really running away with itself. By this time I had learned a little tact so I said nothing, who was I to change the dimensions of their fantasy? I just kept a low profile until I was asked to attend the event as a *guest* of the *guest judges*. It would be a crap night by my usual standards but beggars can't be choosers, I was skint, and a night out was still a night out.

The last two weeks of November came and went, dinner suits and evening dresses were dry cleaned and stay pressed, this was wise because half of being famous was looking famous it wasn't necessarily about talent. (Ask Victoria Beckham).

As they stood on the night in all their evening dress beauty they looked like a million dollars. Tonight they were going to be Mr.& Mrs. Flynn, 'Royalty of Amateur Talent', and no Burton's suit or Dorothy Perkins dress was going to stand in their way.

'Sylvie, you ready?'

'Just a minute'.

Dad paced the living room muttering something under his breath about women getting ready. He was nervous.

'Have you got your speech prepared Dad?'

Dad nodded nonchalantly.

'Of course I have, I've been rehearsing it since last week.'

His face twitched, only a little bit, but it was a twitch all the same. It wasn't worth reacting to because even the best actors or bullshiter's suffer with stage fright.

'Have you got prompting cards?'

'I don't need prompting cards, it's all imprinted in here'.

He said tapping his temple, then he was silent. He rubbed his hands together, all of a sudden prompting cards sounded like a good idea, why hadn't he thought of it? I mean, what was he going to do if he dried up?

'As long as you're sure'

Mum breezed into the room from upstairs.

'How do I look?'

She asked my Father.

'Great, have you got a pen and some cards?'

Mum tutted she could have been naked and he wouldn't have noticed her, but she didn't take offence because she knew how important this night was to him. She walked over and touched the ends of her hair in the mirror, twiddling them with her fingers and thumbs. Today she felt playful.

'Not bad for forty-five am I Mick?'

Dad was looking for the bow tie he'd just taken off and now wanted to put back on again, the suggestion of prompting cards had really rattled his cage for some reason.

'Sylvie! I thought you were getting me a pen and some cards.'

'I thought we were leaving now?'

'We are, we are, I just need to take down so notes. Relax and put some make-up on.'

My Mother protested.

'But I'm already made up'.

'Then put some more on'. He cracked back, and then *we all* knew to shut up and joke no more.

In the car journey to the Warden Bay Hotel everything started to calm down a bit. The cards and pen had been located, and as we travelled Mum scribbled out notes on the same cards to my Father's diction. It was great theatre watching those two, because in front of my very eyes the judging at this talent show had become nothing short of an awards ceremony. 'Ladies and gentlemen' this, and 'right honourable' that, 'I would like to thank' him, 'I would like to commiserate' her, Brilliant.

'What's this place like anyway Dad?'

My Father cleared his throat, a caesura before a lie.

'Well it's been there for many years but don't be put off by that?' The Warden Bay is spoken of in high places'.

'So it's shabby then?'

'Working class!'

This was my Mother's verbal ace whenever I decided to knock something she had a love of. It was a short sentence designed to remind me of who I was, and what I should be proud of. I'm not a snob but through my Mother's over use of this phrase I always associated 'make do and mend' with 'working class', and when I got to the Warden Bay Hotel I wasn't disappointed. Basically it was a large pub that'd had a café stuck on the side, and then an amusement arcade slapped onto that. I could see that with its prime location onto a heavily polluted beach it would have been incredibly popular in the sixties when companies still had annual jamborees. I could see them now , throwing up and arguing as 'Pete the factory foreman' slugged it out with two boys from the stores department.

'Is this it?' I joked.

'It's lovely inside.' My Mother enthused, I doubted that, I was sure that the interior would speak the same volumes as the exterior.

'Sylvie, have you got the cards?'

'They're in my handbag'.

'Are they in order?'

My Mother patted his hand for comfort.

'Of course they are, relax, you're going to be fine'.

I made a sign of the cross in the backseat so he could see it in the rear view mirror, I know this wasn't a particularly supportive thing to do, but there again things weren't particularly sane at that moment either, *'Tonight Matthew I'm going to be Terry Wogan'*.

'Good luck Dad, break a leg'.

It was the most credible thing I could think of saying.

'That's a fine thing to say, fancy wishing a broken limb on your Father.'

I didn't bother explaining, it was pointless explaining the word 'cliché' to a woman who saw the world in black and white, so I just apologised and wished him luck nicely.

I know I haven't built it up very well but I've got to say that the inside of the Warden Bay Hotel *was* marginally better than the outside, less dog shit anyway.

For one thing, it *was* clean, *and* spacious. I liked the way that the cracks were cleverly hidden with stone cladding and poor lighting, just like I adored the photograph of the Queen Mum above the bar, in a strange type of way it all fitted together. My Mother and Father entered and were immediately welcomed by the owner who showed them to a private table. A giggle was shared between the three of them and I left for the bar because sherry and vol-a-vonts weren't my scene. I ordered my first pint and sunk it in seconds hoping that the quickness of my consumption would drown the noise of the children running around destroying anything that wasn't nailed down. I don't blame them though it wasn't their faults, I realised solid role models would be missing from their lives when I saw their parents at the bar smothered in gold talking stolen goods. Somebody tapped the microphone.

'Ladies and gentlemen welcome to the Warden Bay Hotel, tonight is cabaret night'.

The crowd cheered.

'We're going to be starting in about ten minutes so if you'd all like to grab a drink at the bar and then take your seats it would be much appreciated'.

The whole room moved, men went to the bar and women shuffled tables, putting coats on chairs as they hounded their tribes together. Grandparents went to the toilets afraid that they wouldn't be able to hold on, and barmen rushed about scooping up empties. Then the microphone was tapped again.

'Ladies and gentlemen we have a little lost girl at the bar called Tracy, she's looking for her Mummy,

'Bab's'. If 'Babs' could contact Roy behind the bar he'll take you to the store room where she's being kept'.

Poor old Bab's she was probably worried sick, she'd have to gulp her Malibu and Coke now. Not as sick as the owners would be when they'd realised they'd been scammed by 'Tracy the midget beer thief', a teenager from Chatham who specialised in alcoholic collusion. (Just a joke, Tracy was reunited with Babs, and Babs's common law partner Bill, himself on the run and also distressed)

Just before curtain up my parents slipped off backstage to meet all of the competitors who'd mutinied the toilets as their changing rooms. This wasn't a public relations exercise, this was work! Wanting things to run smoothly, they inspected numbers on costumes, paper work, and the pronunciation of the Chinese dancing squad. These two were consummate professionals from beginning to end.

I sunk another two pints and wobbled, this cheap beer was nasty, I must remember to get a drop of lime in the next pint.

Mum ran past me on the way to the loo, nerves had got the best of her bladder.

'How's it going Mum?' I slurred. She stopped dead in her tracks.

'*How much have you had to drink?*'

'Not much, just a couple.'

I wished I'd said nothing, but it was lonely standing up here with two dozen Bob Hoskins sound-a-likes.

'Well make sure you don't show your Father up'.

She was speaking quite loudly now and that was dangerous in a place like this so I moved her to one side to pacify her.

'*Will you calm down*, nobody's going to show anybody up. I'm here to support you.'

She smiled, it was all she wanted to hear. I guess fame had got to her a bit and it would take a while for her to find her feet.

'Okay, we've reserved you a chair by us, why don't you bring your drink and sit down.'

'Yeah I will in a minute.'

This was a blatant lie, my only intention was to prop the bar up all night and maybe consume a packet of peanuts or two. If I sat next to Mr. and Mrs. 'Hyper' I knew I'd end up rowing with them. Off she trotted to the toilets.

'Is your Mother one of the judges?'

I turned round to see a beautiful girl with flowing red hair and a silver face. Her body was dressed in what I could only describe as a badly fitting Elvis suit made out of tin foil, but her figure was heavenly. I know I'd had a few pints by then but something told me she was a competitor, maybe it was the silver face or maybe it was her coned bacofoil breasts that gave it away.

'I'm sorry?'

'I wondered if that lady judge was your Mother?'

'Oh yes that's my Mother all right.'

We both looked at one another, what did she want? An autograph or something? Normally I avoided drunken conversation but in my current state of loneliness I decided to exchange the kind of conversation you shouldn't when you've had too much to drink.

'I like your outfit, are you performing tonight?'

'Oh yes, we're on second, a dance troupe called 'Taboo'.

I looked at her with her silver face and wondered how attractive she was underneath that paint and bullshit.

'Well if you're on second I'll have to remind my parents to watch your act *very* closely.'

The girl jumped for joy, in her own mind she now had an advantage over every other person in the show, she was *in* with the judges.

'Will you be watching too?'

'Of course I will, why don't we have a drink afterwards, *you know*, to celebrate your success.'

I winked at her, the whole thing was so leading it was sickening, perverts like me with four pints of lager in their bellies should be locked up for their own safety. Who was I to imply that *my word* would help her objective, I might as well have laid on a casting couch with my legs apart. My Dad walked over and the girl with the silver face skipped off not wanting to make her advantage public knowledge.

'Whose that?'

'Act two.'

My Father sniggered.

'I thought I remembered her, she was part of a dancing act in the semi-finals.'

He paused.

'Shouldn't have been there really, shameless the positions they get into.'

Bang went my quiet word, poor old silver face would be lucky to place tenth now. My Father coughed and cleared his throat.

'I've come over here on the advice of your Mother.'

I could see he was ill at ease with the topic.

'She thinks you're knocking the booze back too quickly.'

'*She what?*'

'Calm down, she just doesn't want you being ill or anything, *you are* only seventeen.'

Typical! She wasn't happy with chastising me herself she had to involve everyone as well. That's what I hated about parents. I mean, they were quite prepared to stand there and quote the ten commandments, but they were never prepared to admit that they were doing much worse at my age. I bet those two were out every night at seventeen, pissing their working class education's up the wall to the theme of Sergeant Peppers, and here they were begrudging me a couple of pints. Well I wasn't going to stand for it, why should I? My Father walked off and I ordered another pint. The lights dipped.

'Ladies and gentlemen can I have your attention please.'

The noise of the audience simmered to a murmur.

'Tonight we have two very special people to judge our grand final, Ladies and gentlemen from the world of boxing let me introduce our special guest judges for tonight, Mr. and Mrs. Amateur boxing, Bernie and Sylvie Flynn.'

The crowd roared with support, 'pub singers of the world unite' I thought, what was I doing here?

Mum and Dad took their seats and the show kicked off with Danny Bloom and his amazing Paul Anka impression. According to the rules each singing act was only allowed to perform three songs each, as luck would have it poor old Danny Bloom only knew two, so for his final piece he just sang his first song acoustically again. On MTV this would be praised but here at the Warden Bay the crowd felt cheated. As Danny strummed the opening chords of 'Diana' for a second time the crowd booed, not stopping until he finished.

Next on was Taboo, the female dancing trio that sort of placed the Karma Sutra to hip-hop. I liked it but the family crowd was unsure, and after all they were the real judges of this event. I have to be fair it wasn't that bad but I knew it was doomed when I saw the women in the crowd covering their children's eyes. I guess in the sleepy Isle of Sheppy it was just too risky for children who hadn't passed through puberty yet, but for sad people like me, it was nice to see women slithering over one another. The music came to a close and the girls slipped off the stage to their cosmic changing room in the ladies toilet. I stood unfazed as any man could be sporting an erection, I'd never fantasised about tin foil and cooking fat before.

Act three started and the crowd soon forgot acts one and two as this new duo worked their way through a medley of Chas 'n' Dave numbers, three minutes in show business is an extremely long time. I stood there and took the whole thing in, wondering about the conversations my parents would be having about Danny Bloom and the alluring Taboo. Then I saw her stroll over out the corner of my eye.

'What did you think?'
'Absolutely fantastic.'
'*Really?*'

I painted my most honest face.

'Of course, you were fantastic. Didn't you hear the crowd afterwards?'

She jumped up and down with joy, her breasts like two puppies in a sack. She winked.

'Did you get a chance to speak to the judges?'

'Of course, and *I know* they loved your act as much as I did, they remembered you from the semi-final you know.'

Silver face leaned over and kissed me on the cheek and I decided to lay my sexist cards on the table.

'Look it's a bit hot in here, do you fancy a walk outside?'

She grinned.

'Of course we can go for a walk, but let me take this costume off first it's cold outside.'

She kissed me on the cheek again this time more passionately, we both agreed to reconvene our little chat outside the hotel in five minutes time. My Father peered over at me and gave me one of those knowing glances that said, 'dirty swine'. The only problem that faced me now was going to the toilet without passing my parents who'd become Quakers in regards to my alcohol consumption. I *was* pissed though, and as much as I'd enjoyed the thought of it, I didn't want any parental aggravation. So, with a final burst of logic before my conscious mind shut down I decided not to use the toilet in the Warden Bay Hotel. To use that toilet would have involved walking past my parents at the judge's table. No, I was going to be smart and avoid the whole confrontation thing by taking a leak outside.

I stumbled across the room nudging a table of drinks as I went. It seemed as if my bladder was going to burst, I may have been alright five minutes ago but I definitely wasn't alright now, I needed to pee and I needed to pee fast.

Outside the cold air caught me and I found myself having the kind of inner dialogue that all drunks have when a shag is imminent. The kind of talk that tells you to calm down and not blow it, it wasn't exactly a moment of truth or anything but it was pretty close. I unzipped my flies with the intention of dispersing a couple of litres of warm urine onto the ground and then realised that I was still too close to the entrance. I may have wanted to go, but I also realised that my parents were inside as guest judges and I didn't want to ruin their evening. I mean, how would it look if someone was to see me and then make a connection with the well dressed dignitaries inside, beetroot wouldn't start to describe the colour.

I ran across the road away from the fairy lights of the Warden Bay Hotel and tried once again to strain my leaks, but it was no good. As the cars swung round the bend of the road their headlights caught the shadow of my one eyed friend and I knew I had to take additional precautions. This wasn't easy, time was running out. My bladder had swelled to the size of an Iranian watermelon and I was crumbling under the pressure, courtesy was once thing but incontinence was another. Then under the Sheppy sunset it came to me. On the beach some ten feet away stood a grassy bank partly constructed to house a new sewerage pipe. My solution was there. I would run to the top of the bank and relieve myself in the most natural of ways, all under the cover of darkness.

Left foot right foot I scrambled to the top of the bank, to finally have the opportunity to pee was an extremely exhilarating experience. Psychologists call this homeostasis; a feeling of warmth experienced throughout the whole body, I just called it 'warm', as I pissed and pissed. As I let it all go I thought, what fantastic joy, what holy elation, balance comes from simple things and here I was happy as a pig in shit, 'Micky Flynn, the amazing beer monster on a piss fest'. Don't get too comfortable though, because this ecstasy was soon to come to a close. As I took a half step forward to extract the final gallon before zipping myself up I shuffled my left foot forward for leverage. I must have stepped on a sodden piece of turf or something, because as I shuffled I slipped, and as I slipped I fell. In my drunken state this was quite distressing, long falls usually end up with a concrete conclusion at the other end. I'd only come out to borrow the loo and now I was faced with being scooped off of the pavement I thought. Maybe lady luck was smiling down on me or maybe I was a cat with nine lives, but that night I wasn't to meet my maker in the velvet skies above. That night I was to fall into an open sewer, not just any open sewer, but an open sewer full of untreated muck. At first I was happy because I thought I'd fallen into a pond, mud's unpleasant but it's certainly not deadly, however this feeling of safety went as quick as it came when I observed the first wave of toilet paper sailing about my ears. Then the stench hit my nostrils and I wished I'd fallen on the concrete pavement. I swam to the edge and struggled back up the bank, shit surrounded my every side its texture so utterly disgusting that I still heave when I think about it today. I got halfway up and slipped back in, my fingernails encrusted with a thousand curries. This was a horrible way to die, 'death by shit', it wouldn't look good on any headstone. I had just about given up hope when I decided to have another go and managed to heave myself out. (In more ways than one.)

At the top of the bank I tried to wipe myself down the best I could, but ended up spreading it around until I resembled a twelve stone turd with two white eyes. It was useless, not even I could talk my way out of this situation. I walked back to the Warden Bay Hotel and past the girl with the silver face who didn't recognise me. When you're in deep shit sometimes the only thing left to do is to say sorry, and by the look of it I had a lot of apologising to do. It was a long walk to the judges table, the only consolation was, that as I entered the room I managed to obtain a larger laugh than the second rate comedian on stage.

'Mum, Dad I'm sorry, I've had a slight accident.'

My Mum screwed her face up, how could this beast possibly be her son? She must have thought that I'd shitted myself to death.

'Mick is that you?'

'Yeah, but I didn't do this on purpose, honest I didn't.'

The place went silent, even the comedian turned his microphone off. Suddenly I was the show. The first person sniggered, then a second, it was like a Mexican wave working its way around the room, soon the whole lounge was in rapturous laughter, all at me. My Father just dipped his head in shame and told my Mother that we were leaving, the final humiliation came from the crowd who clapped us all out.

Outside the hotel my Father made me strip butt naked wrapping me in a roll of Clingfilm that he kept in the boot for emergencies such as this. Normally he wouldn't have been this mercenary but this was a new car and he didn't want to harm the interior before the 'new smell' had subsided. I had ruined everything by getting drunk and falling in shit, and now my parents were too angry to talk to me. Instead of credibility they had received humiliation, their fantasy shattered into a million pieces all because of me.

The journey home was silent apart from the odd huff and sigh I didn't want to push my luck so I didn't start any long conversations, my Father could be an extremely revengeful man. The journey home was quicker that time of night but it was also bumpy and it wasn't long before my bladder filled up again.

'Dad.'

'What?'

'I need to go to the toilet again.

The silence became thicker.

'Can't you wait?' Heckled my Mother still angry at the memory of loosing her fame and becoming a laughing stock.

'I'm sorry Mum, I've got to go again.'

My Father brought the car to a screeching halt, it was the final straw that broke the donkey's back, once again I had pushed them too far.

'Unwrap the Clingfilm, do what you've got to do in the bushes, and then get back in the car.'

His words were stern and cold, I knew when to obey. I slid out of the car and took my wrapper off revealing my nakedness to the world, It was cold here in December.

'Do it in the bushes Mick or you'll be done for exposing yourself.'

He had a point, so still keen to build bridges I ran to the shelter of the hedges. As I checked my footing and took my aim I saw my Father pulling away, that's right, the miserable old bastard was going to leave me there. I ran up the hard shoulder after him begging him for forgiveness, every two hundred yards he'd stop to let me catch up, and then he'd be off again. It was so embarrassing, what if the Police were to turn up? On and on he did this for about a mile, at the point of tears I was given a reprieve and let back in the car. Justice had been done, the remainder of the journey finished in absolute silence.

CHAPTER 8
Loved and Died

I perch next to your sleeping head,
Stroke your locks touch your skin,
God has really blessed me.
You look so peaceful in your rest,
Contented and smooth in dreams,
Alive, so very alive.
You stir and I move back,
I don't want to tear this picture,
This perfect Picasso with sunflower colours.
But don't ever leave me,
Don't ever pass not here without this,
Don't deprive my eyes of you.
The launcher of a billion ships.

Don't smoke cannabis, I know it's relaxing and I know it compliments Bob Dylan, but don't smoke it because it cocks up your reaction time. It's true that under the influence of cannabis one can still operate, I mean we can still make a cup of tea, and we can still pop down the local shop to buy some Pringles. But the more complexed tasks like saving someone's life cannabis smokers seem to have a problem with.

I've got to be honest I've had problems adjusting and who wouldn't? But much as I try to fit in I can't, University is a weird place full of the strangest people. When I started the course I thought I'd get along with everyone, we are all studying the same subjects so I thought we'd all have similar ideas and mindsets. Wrong! Sometimes when I'm in class I look around and become worried that some of these people could possibly become our next generation of managing directors and leaders. We may all be studying at degree level but I tell you this, I've never met a bigger bunch of dunces in my life. Not academically but emotionally.

I know it's my age but in my limited sphere of knowledge I have learned that students love a drama, not little dramas but great big epics where they have to involve every bastard and their Mothers. You can split these people into two categories. There are the people who are nineteen going on forty-seven and the others who are nineteen going on twelve. For most of the students this is their first time away from home so one could argue that this is not their faults, however I do think it's a sorry state of affairs when most of them don't know how to iron their clothes or change a light bulb. Luckily for me I hooked up with some great people, I tended to stay clear of all the others.

One of my best pals in the world is a female bassist who plays in a little trio we have. She's a real complexed character with all the talent of a modern day Mozart. The other member of the band is a guitarist called Pete, an equally fantastic person. I'm not drunk or stoned so I can honestly say this in the cold light of day, these two people especially Hannah (The bassist) are the only reason that I still have my sanity. Friends like these ask for nothing but because of their caring ways you always feel in debt to them, can you imagine my horror when I nearly killed one of them.

People deal with illness in different ways, I tend to go all quiet and lock myself in my room whereas Hannah is a terrible hypochondriac. She can never just have a headache it's has to be a tumour, and when she has got a headache or flu she has to tell you how ill she feels every bloody two minutes. I know this sounds terribly heartless because when people are ill they feel down in the dumps, but you try living with someone like that, believe me it does your bloody head in after a while

It must have been somewhere around the middle of November, Pete, Hannah and I had been busy rehearsing for a gig at a local pub in Pontypridd called, 'The Knot Inn'. I'd only been playing the guitar properly for a couple of years and the thought of actually having people come to hear me play was a frightening contemplation. This aside I was confident though, we had written most of our own songs and the few covers that we did knock out sounded better than the originals in my mind. I'm not a great singer so I was happy for Hannah to take lead vocals for two thirds of the set, that way I could hide behind her and Pete's brilliance. Everything was going great, I was with people I liked, I had a platform for my words and most important there were no arguments. I loved the nights that we got together it was great because it usually involved a couple of beers, a spliff and some cool chat – three of my favourite things.

About three weeks out from D-Day Hannah caught a cold, we carried on rehearsing as normal but she began to get worried. Everytime she hit a high note she cringed complaining of a sore throat, I ignored this because no matter how much she cringed she still sounded good to me. This cringe turned into a moan and then from a moan into a worry.

"What if I loose my voice on the night?" She would say after every song.

"You wont, It's just a cold."

And onwards we would continue making rock and roll history in the front living room of my accommodation. I knew her condition was getting worse because after one rehearsal I could hear her coughing up green muck in the bathroom, then I knew we were in trouble. There was no way I could sing her songs, I just didn't have the vocal range so I convinced myself again that this was just a cold. Poor old Hannah she must have felt really unloved as I shoved vitamin C down her throat by the bottle full, worried that my lack of talent would be exposed by her lack of voice.

"It's just a cold, pull yourself together." I would say over and over hoping that she too would actually start to believe it, but she wasn't getting better and both Pete and I began to get nervous. Then one day in the middle of a session she stopped mid-way through a song and sat down complaining of a sore throat. I knew that December 12th was not going to happen.

"What's a matter?"

"My throat, it's on fire."

Pete looked at me I knew what he was thinking so we stopped playing, it was useless pushing someone who really wasn't well enough to continue.

"Let's call it a night, maybe you'll feel better in the morning."

This was a good call by Pete, after all, we all knew the songs, we'd played them a million times each, and besides, we had a couple of bottles of wine to finish in the kitchen as well as a lump of hash. Hannah slumped down in the armchair she looked incredibly pale and sickly, the surface of her skin had taken an unhealthy sweaty sheen, even I stopped being an inconsiderate bastard for a second.

"Are you alright?"

Brave to the last she squeezed out a smile.

"I could murder something to drink."

I patted her supple thigh, it wasn't a sexual suggestion, more of a comforting pat aimed to make her feel better.

"Sure, what do you want red or white wine?"

"Just water." She whispered. "I'm so thirsty."

I tiptoed into the kitchen and ran the tap so it was cold and returned with the glass of water as Pete poured our tumblers of red wine. Hannah gulped from the glass and asked for some more.

"Let me have a look at your tonsils if your throat is sore."

Hannah opened her mouth and I had a look in, not that I knew what I was looking for.

"What can you see?" She gurgled.

"nothing, it's too dark."

Pete passed me his lighter it was the closest thing we had to a torch in the house.

"Roll us a doobie while I have a look at Hannah's tonsils."

Pete put his wine down and set out a three-skinner, weed is a major student occupation. I struck up the lighter and had a look inside Hannah's mouth, it was worse than I thought.

"Oi Pete, have a look at this."

Pete continued rolling.

"Why?"

I didn't want to say that poor old Hannah here was sporting a pair of tonsils the size of golf balls in case she'd flip out, but I tell you this. I've looked inside a few mouths in my time, and to this day I've never seen anything more ugly or more worrying in my life. Firstly they were big, real big, and secondly they were 'veiny'. The kind of equipment that every man would ideally like to have in their pants but not in their throats. Pete finished rolling the joint and came over to have a peak at Hannah and her amazing tonsils. Unfortunately he wasn't as tactful as me.

"Fuck me, they shouldn't look like that should they?"

Hannah let out a moan. "What's wrong with them?"

"Nothing, they're just a little big that's all why don't I get you a hot drink or something?"

I had really grown to hate the house I was in, it had been nothing but unlucky for me right from the start. The location was okay just like my room was okay, but two of the three people I lived with drove me crazy. I'm not going to pretend that I'm easy to live with because I'm not, but I've never been overpowering in the way that they were. Maybe you've met people like this, ones whose favourite subjects are themselves, and the same ones who speak over everything else that doesn't include them. It would be okay if I could escape this but I can't. As soon as they are on their own they barge into my room seeking a conversation about a bloody text message or something. This is okay for the first half a dozen times but it does piss you off when it affects your sleep at 1am.

I took the joint with me and went to the kitchen to make her a cup of tea. I stuck the kettle on the stove and lit the gas as Pete shouted through, 'How long.'s that tea taking.'

'Hold your horses I've just lit the gas.'

I hated this kettle it took ages to boil, why couldn't we just have an electric one like the rest of the nation? I'll tell you why, because the landlady's daughter said so, that's why. In her infinite wisdom of all things cool she'd decided that these boil-on-the-stove kettles were all the rage and therefore bestowed one upon the house, and now I have to wait ten minutes for a cup of tea. This girl I shared the house with which made slagging the landlady off very difficult, something that all students like to do. As a character she was alright I suppose, well, until she opened her mouth. Some people curse and some people are racist, but this girl had an opinion on nothing. Ask her a question and you'd wait ten days for an answer, ask her about something from 'Cosmo' and she'd repeat the article back to you word for word. These are the most dangerous of people because their ethos of life is based solely around what they're told to believe and not what they experience.

The kettle boiled, it had to eventually. I poured the hot liquid into a cup and made a brew. As a rule Hannah didn't take sugar but I stuck a couple in there anyway figuring that the sweetness might help get rid of some of that horrible yellow stuff coating her tonsils.

"Where's that spliff?"

Pete moaned. I smiled.

"Stop moaning and roll another one."

As helpful as ever Pete complied wetting his lips for the second time that evening.

"There you go Hannah, don't gulp it too quickly, it's hot."

Hannah said thank-you, as always I was humbled by her courtesy. I kissed her forehead.
"You'll be alright."
For the first time since we started playing as a band I stopped thinking about the music and started thinking about the members. These two people, especially Hannah were the first two people ever to listen to me in the way I wanted to be listened to. I'd had friends before and I'd also had a great wife but I'd never had the guts to tell these people everything about me. Hannah had been there when I'd cried, she had listened to my endless ramblings and made me laugh with drunken gymnastic displays. There were nights when we talked about everything for twelve hours or more, what can I say? She knew me warts and all. It wasn't just her listening skills that made her alluring though. She was an amazing person, she had strong opinions but managed to never judge anyone or anything. Hannah just glided over the surface of things like silk on your face, never hurting anyone. So you can imagine how saddened I was when I didn't know how to help her.
"Do you want some on this?"
Pete leaned over and passed me the joint.
As concerned as I was for Hannah's condition nothing got between students and *the* smoke, at this time in my life getting blitzed was as close as I could get to tuning out from reality. Normally I hated excess, I had a family full of alcoholics that I'd never understood, so as a rule I'd tried to stay away from anything addictive. I wasn't being judgmental or anything it was just that 'excess' had always seemed such a terrible waste to me. All that was different now, when I split up with Karen a

little piece of me died, dying was something I didn't want to face. Dying meant the end and I wanted to prove to everyone that I could still do it on my own, I wanted to show them that I didn't have to stick to sixty years of nine to five just to be successful. My parents had done that and look how bitter they were. So I took the easy option, an option that was in my mind a shortcut, I used alcohol and drugs to escape. Not a noble thing but then I've never considered myself a hero regardless of how brave my parents think I am. Being a drug user you might find it strange that I don't advocate drug use, nor do I think it should be legalised but let me tell you this, cannabis is a great numbing agent when you feel like crap, and that's what I used it for. I know that I'm going to have to give it up because on drugs you have a limited existence but for now I'm happy to be in denial, for some reason I think it's safer.

Anyway, as the night crept on one joint turned into six or seven and two bottles of wine turned into four, by nine o' clock Pete and I were happy in oblivion. Poor Hannah just sat there in her own oblivion nursing what turned out to be glandular fever.

"My throat feels worse."

I stopped not knowing what else to do, in the last two days Hannah had consumed every throat lozenge on the face of the planet as well as a fair supply of cough mixture. Then I remembered the time that I'd had tonsillitis when I was fourteen and how it was cured. I too had been a victim of this cursed illness and had canned my condition with half a pint of vodka, maybe we could do the same for her.

"Don't worry Hanz, I've got something that'll sort you out."

She smiled believing in whatever miracle cure I was about to concoct, anything was better than what she was feeling now. I stumbled into the kitchen looking for vodka but couldn't find any. So I opened the cupboard of my other housemate, a Bristolian girl with a weird fetish for self-absorption. Her favourite subject was *her*self, a topic she would love to bore me with for hours on end. To this day I don't know why she had such a love of herself because up to this point in my life she stands as the most transparent character I've ever met. An ugly girl inside and out with the morals of a weasel and all the intelligence of Forrest Gump. As ugly and stupid as she was, she still had a healthy supply of Drambuie, and if I didn't have vodka then Drambuie would do instead. So that's what I did, I took her bottle of Drambuie and poured out a beaker full taking it to the dying Hannah in the lounge.

"Drink that!"

"What?"

She said, puzzled by the drink I'd brought her.

"Drink this quick and I promise it'll make your throat feel better."

She frowned, Hannah had faith but she wasn't stupid.

"What is it?"

"Drambuie."

I said. "Won't that make me ill?"

I sighed, she either wanted a cure or she didn't.

'It won't be nice, but *it will* cleanse your throat. This stuff is pure spirit, I've seen John Wayne do something similar in a film.'

Hannah winced, she didn't want to upset me by telling me to stick my miracle, because at that moment in time she would have tried anything to feel better. Besides, there was no physical way I was going to be able to pour the liquor back into the bottle, excess Cannabis makes your hands shake. She took the glass, tears welling up in her eyes, in some perverted way she had passed the point of no return.

'That's it, go on, knock it back.'

She pressed the glass to her lips, opened her mouth wide and gulped the contents. For a split second her face took on a look of peace. This peace was quickly replaced with a frown of horror as she coughed and choked her was through the remainder of the miracle cure. Pete giggled and then I did too, even tough guys joked. I patted the hollow of her back.

"There that's better isn't it?"

Hannah shook her head furiously, she was in trouble. Pete stopped laughing and I did too, suddenly my stoned fun didn't seem funny anymore. I whacked her back again confident that this would dislodge any foreign body stuck I her throat. Hannah opened her mouth to say something but no words came out. Pete stumbled over, if Hannah died our actions would make him an accessory to murder and he still had two years of a degree to finish.

"What's up with her?"
"I don't know."

Hannah's eyes were closing she was loosing consciousness, this often happens when people can't breathe even I know that.

"Hit her again."

"*I've already done that.*"

The paranoia from the cannabis was now kicking in strong.

"Well do it harder."

I whacked her back again with my fist, and this time she was able to take a proper mouthful of air. How could I have been so stupid?

"Quick, stick her in the recovery position." Said Pete.

"Hold on let's wait a minute."

I guess Pete's paranoia was kicking in too, but right now all we needed to relax and celebrate the fact that Hannah was still alive before deciding upon our next course of action. Damn this cannabis! If I had a clear head now I'd know what to do, if I had a clear head I would come up with one of those solutions that the landlady's daughter would only dream about. Fuck! I was such an idiot, why did I let myself get into such a state? I'll tell you why, I got into these states because I couldn't cope, because running was easier that standing still seeing what a joke my life had become. Twenty-nine, no qualifications stuck in a 'bed-sit' in a run down valley town. I would have talked to someone about it if I'd had the chance, but the one thing I'd learned this year was that no one really gave a toss, here, or back at the marital home. They just saw a guy with a few interesting stories, probably never thought someone like me could've wanted more, something more than money or fame, but they were wrong. I wanted to live, to taste the zest of doing something holy, something hallowed that would make me proud. That's right me, no one else, me. So I opted out, and what did they do, that's right, rather than try to understand me they condemned me, sent me to Coventry blaming it on some mutated mid life crisis at twenty-nine. Well fuck them, fuck them all! I may not be happy but I am honest, at least I wouldn't be a bitter old man in a rocking chair moaning about all the things I could have been. I was here on the sharp end trying to reach some invisible potential even if that did mean sacrificing my sanity along the way.

"Let's ask Hannah what she wants Pete."

She probably had more suggestions than us anyway.

"What should we do Hannah?"

"Call a doctor." She whispered. "Just call a doctor, I feel so ill."

I was wasted so I went the whole hog and called 999, if it was a false alarm then they could bill me for the costs and add it to my other debts. As it happened it was the right thing to do for that night the emergency services admitted Hannah into the Royal Glamorgan hospital for ten days on a course of strong anti-biotics and steroids. The paramedic who arrived on the scene was to say that he'd never seen a pair of tonsils so large in all his life. I'm not going to blow the whole thing out of proportion but that night actually made me think for the first time about what I was doing to myself and how I had to start moving forward. Hannah's condition had materialised out of my lack of concern and worry for others, and for that I am still ashamed, thank Jehovah she's *still* alive.

MY PILES

'Never trust the doctors' always sounded like one of those battle cries that never made sense. Why shouldn't I trust the doctors? I mean, they study for seven years, then they have two years as a trainee and when they do qualify they're watched by an independent organisation. I've been to a few places on this planet and I can tell you that although the NHS make mistakes they still stand as the best of the best. Now I'm not supporting poor performance who would? But the problem lies in the business in which they work and not with the personnel themselves. If someone makes a mistake in an insurance office we think nothing of it, but if a doctor makes a mistake it usually involves a death, so naturally people kick up fuss. In bad cases they phone the press who see a sales opportunity and before we know it everyone's up in arms slagging off the health service. I say it again! I do not support poor performance, if someone acts in an irresponsible way that causes death or disablement, they should be punished. Likewise is anyone's upset with the service in anyway they should speak up, but for God's sake don't write off the whole service because if we're not careful we're going to have an environment like America. You know what I'm talking about, we've all seen at least one episode of ER where doctors are apprehensive to complete certain operations for fear of liable. Please let's not get like that.

I sound like a real hero don't I? Standing here singing up the merits of the NHS. I bet there's a few readers saying 'I bet he's never been in hospital' Well you're wrong I have, and do you want to know something else, my visit was a disaster too, but I still think they're the best medical staff in the world. So now we're straight, let me tell you about my hospital visit and the events leading up to it.

I was twenty-two with money in my pocket, money and youth is always a dangerous combination, a bit like fuel and fire if you ask me. You see at twenty-two you couldn't tell me anything, in my little world of flash cars and designer underpants I knew everything about everything. Why should I listen to anyone else? I had a house a wife and a good job, and most importantly no worries. In the nineties people like me were called 'DINKS'–double income no kids, and boy did I love it. It frightens me to think that back then Karen and I wouldn't even bat an eyelid at wasting a hundred pounds plus on our weekly shopping bill. Especially now when I consider twenty-fives pounds a week excessive on food 'substances'. I use the word 'substances' because the Tesco value range rarely contains anything in its ingredients that can loosely be defined as food. (No liable action please, it's just a joke)

Anyway one week I got a call at work from my school hood pal Dave Parr (The same guy involved in the fumbling rings scam) inviting me on an all night bender at Sandgate Rowing club. It wasn't the most kicking place in Kent but the surroundings were clement and the beer was cheap, so when the invite hit the mat I was happy at the chance for some old fashioned male bonding. Sandgate was a great area because it was too upper class to be considered Folkestone, but not quite affluent enough to be seen as Hythe, so it suited me fine. When I was a teenager Sandgate was the type of place you took your girlfriend for a drink, quaint pubs done out like the insides of boats and snug little coffee shops that never seemed to close.

I jumped into my car with the go faster stripes and headed off down to the coast. To be honest I was far too old for the kind of teenage frivolity that Dave and I would usually get up to but I just couldn't stop myself. The chance to get away from it all with a nutter who just knew no bounds was too much of an allure for a 'DINK' with money in his pocket.

"So what we drinking?"

Dave threw his arms around me and gave me a big hug.

"You made it."

"Of course I made it."

Dave ran and got his little brother Paul, I say little but he was six foot four now.

"Look who it is."

Paul gave me a hug too it was all male dominated but innocent enough, we'd been through the greedy eighties, so a hug between guys was okay.

"Here have this."

Dave said thrusting a pint of cloudy muck into my grubby mitts.

"What is it?"

"It's a new drink called Newquay Steam Bitter, you'll love it."

I've never been a great drinker, that didn't mean I didn't enjoy it, it just that I've never really been able to hold it. To explain this I'll have to plagiarise the lyrics of a famous eighties song, 'You'd always find me in the kitchen at parties.' I was the type of person who'd go to a party at seven and be plastered by seven forty five in the kitchen looking for my friends. My downfall was gulping. I could never just enjoy the beer that was in my glass, I'd always have to worry about the beer that was left in the barrel. I'd knock back cans like a chain smoker would consume cigarettes, maybe it was that famous self destruct gene that had always been prevalent in my family, I don't know.

"Is it strong Dave?"

"Of course it's strong now get it down you."

How could I tell him 'no', how could I say I'll have a Fosters-top instead? I couldn't, so I took the glass and gulped until it was gone. When that was finished I was given another, and another. I tried to eat two packs of crisps to try and soak the beer up but things were moving too fast for me to eat them.

The next twenty-four hours were a bit hazy. I remember going to a club, I remember an awful kebab, and I remember being refused entry into a wine bar called 'Gees'. Then at somewhere around 2am I remember being horrendously sick up someone's steps. In the morning Karen as reliable as ever phoned at 9am she thought I sounded terrible.

"What were you drinking?"

"Newquay Stream Bitter."

She laughed.

"Isn't that a little strong for someone like you?"

Of course it was too strong for someone like me but I didn't need her telling me that.

'When are you coming home?'

'By lunchtime' I said.

Back at our house I became obsessed with the need to throw up again, my wrecked system didn't want or need the chemicals I had lovingly pumped into it over the last twenty four hours, so out they came. Waves of emotion, cries of help as I 'chundered' thirty pounds worth of mistreatment down the pan, a moments worth of peace passed and the vomiting frenzy was replaced with the need to pass motion. It was one of those pains that you couldn't ignore, if you did, you faced the risk of an accident in your pants.

Usually I enjoy the act of 'floating a biscuit' but this time it was different, firstly there was the pain, an intense stabbing sensation that bought tears to my eyes, and secondly there was the blood.

I checked the pan and horrified, it looked like someone had attacked my 'chalfonts' with a chainsaw. Not usually one to cause a commotion I called my wife for a second opinion, (It's the kind of thing that's permitted when you've been married for a couple of years) Karen perused the carnage down below.

You'll have to go to hospital, this isn't right."

I was glad she made the suggestion, being a man you don't usually like to make an admission like that, admitting you're ill is a bit like admitting you're gay.

"It's probably nothing but I'll go all the same."
"Okay."

She said and handed me a feminine panty liner. What did I want with that?

"Put this in your pants."

I laughed, I thinking Karen was humouring me, but she wasn't, she was deadly serious.

"I mean it, put it in your pants, you don't want to be spoiling your suit trousers do you?"

She obviously hadn't thought this through, I place that thing in my pants and true, it would protect my trousers, but what happens at the other end when a male nurse takes it out? I'd be the laughing stock of the hospital. I screwed my face up, there was no way I was putting a fanny rag anywhere near my backside.

"Karen, you can put that thing down *right now* I'm not wearing it!"

She smiled realising the situation from my point of view, but *I was* wearing a Nickleby's hand-finished suit, and for the sake of a bit of embarrassment she wouldn't have it ruined.

"Put that in your pants *now*!"

I may have been bleeding to death but we still managed to argue about it for twenty minutes or more, fighting our sides of money verses embarrassment. The conclusion of our debate come in the form of a compromise, I would wear a pair of tracksuit bottoms with a thin layer of toilet paper, but I wouldn't wear anything with wings.

After signing in and waiting four hours I was seen by a doctor. A nice chap who probably hadn't slept for about seventy-two hours, but still humorous. I suppose when you spend a proportion of your working day seeing those sides of people that you'd rather not see, the only thing you have left is your sense of humour.

Funny when I think of it now, but not once did he make eye contact with me during the whole examination. Instead he had the whole conversation with my arse.

"I can see you're a bit messy down there, yes, you look very sore."

This was a strange sensation because I got the feeling he was expecting something from me. I don't know what, maybe he was hoping my arse would talk or something

"Well Mr. Flynn, I can tell you this, it's nothing nasty."

Karen and I sighed in relief.

"But I'd like to keep you in for observation anyway, and perhaps place a camera up your back passage tomorrow if that's alright?"

My face registered horror, no it wasn't alright. No one was ramming a Polaroid instamatic up my Kyber Pass.

'Oh Mr. Flynn don't look so worried it's no ordinary camera, this camera is no bigger than the tip of your finger. We just get some lubricating jelly and pop it up your bottom. It's really quite simple, you can watch it on a screen if you want.'

Maybe it was simple for him but I preferred the image of the Polaroid camera, this was beginning to sound like a bizarre Swedish porno film where half way through the nurse would rip open her top and bring in a troupe of midgets juggling dildo's.

'Will it hurt?'

The doctor laughed.

'Oh no, a bit uncomfortable that's all.'

I wanted to ask if I could keep the videotape afterwards because these things tended to resurface if you ever make it big. Looking up my arse was one thing but having it on a television screen was a no no. I looked at Karen for support but she just looked numb, in instances around doctors she was never very good.

'Have you got any idea what it could be doctor?'

'Not yet, we'll run some blood tests tonight, if we find anything it might mean some minor surgery, but we'll cross that bridge when we come to it'. That was it! Karen burst into tears. Twenty-five years of repressed strength flowed out through the tear ducts in her eyes. It took the doctor and I by surprise, we didn't quite know what to do. I got up from the table and gave her a hug.

'What's a matter?' She wailed.

'I don't want you to die.'

The doctor picked up his clipboard and took control of the situation.

'Mrs. Flynn I assure you Mr. Flynn is not going to die it's just a routine examination,'

He paused and changed the tone of his voice.

'I do a thousand of these a year. Now come on dry your eyes, I'll get some tissues from the other room.'

The doctor kindly left the room leaving Karen and I to talk, in instances like these three was definitely a crowd, a space like this would allow a misogynist man like myself the arena to comfort his wife in private. She sniffed a bit, '*hospital*' was a word she didn't like just like '*camera*' was a word I didn't like. I hated seeing her cry so I thought it prudent to calm the situation down. Yes I was worried about my own well being, but I was also worried about hers. I didn't want to picture her at home crying over old photographs. I was coming back and I wanted her to be my strength.

'Come on Karen, it'll be okay you heard the doctor.'

She smiled through glassy eyes, the same smile you'd give a condemned man as they made their way to the gallows.

'I Know, I just hate hospitals that's all.'

I squeezed her hand tightly this wasn't the environment for someone like her who had no faith in the National Health Service. If I wasn't careful her fear of doctors would transfer itself to me and I'd be the one believing that fifty percent of people who entered these establishments never came out again.

'Look, why don't you get yourself home. They're going to be wheeling me through for my blood tests any minute and you've got an early start in the morning.'

She sniffed a little more and then wished me luck before leaving, she'd be alright she'd probably phone her Dad who'd tell her to pull herself together.

Blood tests and a sleepless night followed, I was woken twice by nurses offering me sleeping pills, what did they teach these girls at college? Waking me up to offer me a sleeping pill was like offering me a laxative if I had dysentery. After saying 'no' I settled again until about 4am, when the old man next to me breathed his last whilst urinating the bed, poor old sod. Morning came and went but I wasn't allowed anything to eat in case they had to operate, tired and hungry didn't place me in the best of moods when the doctor finally got to me at eleven.

'*How long am I going to be here?*'

Was the first thing out of my mouth. The doctor took my temperature and scribbled something down on his pad of paper.

'Now, now Mr. Flynn we've got quite a backlog. We might not be able to sort everything out today. Why is there a problem?'

Apart from no sleep and the man dying next to me there was no problem at all, I won't even think about my hunger. He probably banged two nurses before starting work this morning, *probably* in the back of his vintage roadster with the wire wheels and leather interior. Well he didn't have a bleeding ass and mournful wife at home, he didn't have the Monday reports waiting for him on his desk at work.

'No not a problem as such....'

He interrupted

'Your blood tests came back clear, no real problems there.'

He flicked through his papers some more and I grew impatient.

'It's just that I've got a lot of things to do, and I'd really be appreciative if someone could help me out. You know, place me somewhere up near the front of the queue.'

The doctor winked, an innocent gesture between two professionals. He knew the score, we were both busy men.

'You want to be seen as soon as possible? I'll see what I can do.'

Ten minutes later Karen called to see if I'd had a goodnight, I didn't want to burden her with my worries so I lied.

'Fine, they reckon I'll be out in the next few hours, nothing's shown up on my blood tests.'

Karen wailed. 'That means it's something serious then.'

'Honestly there's nothing wrong, they've just to have a quick look around and then I'm out. Please don't cry.'

Karen's emotion came grinding to a halt as the practical side of her nature kicked in.

'Okay, but give me a call when you want picking up. I don't want you being a martyr and catching the bus or anything, that wont impress anyone Mick.'

Happy to have her back on track was a blessing I didn't want to ruin. I told her I loved her and then told her to get back to work as we needed some spending money for our forthcoming holiday. As soon as I put the phone down the doctor was back, sporting a different coloured clipboard, the sleepy man of earlier was gone.

'Mr. Flynn a doctor can see you now.'

I got up to move.

'Great which way is it?'

'Don't worry about that, I'll have you wheeled down to the student facility.'

He went to leave but I called him back.

'Did you say 'student facility?'

'Yes yes, don't worry. You will be examined by a qualified doctor, it's just that you might have some observers too.'

He went to move away again but I wanted answers. It was my ass, and under the patients charter I had a right to know what was happening to it.

'Hold on a minute, what do you mean observers?'

The doctor lost his patience.

'Mr. Flynn, I'm a busy man. You asked me to get you the earliest examination possible and I've done that. It's nothing out of the ordinary, you'll be examined by a qualified doctor and a couple of students, now please, I have other people to see. Good day.'

Ignorant silver spooned swine, no bedside manner that was his problem.   Couldn't he see that my frustrations were fuelled by nothing more than worry? Someone from across the ward shouted,

'That told him mate.'

'Shut your face.' I shouted back. I was a high bracket wage earner I paid for this service in tax, so in hindsight the doctor worked for me. He had no right to say he was busy, he should be busy with my problems and mine alone. Of course I wouldn't have had this conversation at BUPA, oh no, at BUPA I'd be a VIP lavished with attention, sipping fine wines and eating smoked salmon. I rang the bell. A threesome of ugly nurses arrived in stereo. I wanted to ask after their sister Cinderella but this rudeness could slow up my escape.

'I have an examination at the student facility, I believe there should be someone here to wheel me down.'

The three nurses looked at me in an uninterested manner, the same aura they would've projected as they emptied bedpans I thought.

'Yes, we'll have a word with doctor when he's back.'

I wasn't about to take that, it was too vague, too abstract, for all I knew I might not see the doctor for another twenty-four hours.

"Look according to the Mail on Sunday last week, for every nurse there is on the floor there are three administrators behind the scenes. Now surely between the twelve of you one of you can pick up the telephone and organise an anal examination?" The three nurses looked uncomfortable they were not used to the same confrontational environments as me, they were more used to lonely old men thanking them for a nice stay. The only people they took this kind of stick from was pompous doctors, and they only took that because they saw it as something almost romantic. Like all airhostesses want to marry pilots, nurses also want to marry doctors.

'Mr. Flynn, I can assure you that everyone is working flat out in this hospital.'

'Everyone except you three that is.'

The three nurses looked at one another, it was like the three bloody wise monkey's.

'There's no need to be rude Mr. Flynn.'

They were right of course being rude was unacceptable, but when people are apathetic to someone's plight, and when you're kept out of the communication chain you get annoyed.

'I'm sorry you feel I'm being rude, I just want to know what's going on. I thought you nurses were supposed to be people persons.'

They all huffed, then the smallest nurse on the left spoke up.

'Come on girls we don't have to take this, let's leave Mr. Flynn and his black cloud alone.'

The three of them turned and marched to the reception desk at the end of the ward I could almost hear myself being labelled. They spoke in a hushed manner and then one of them picked up the telephone and made a call. Foolishly I wanted to think that this call was for my benefit but the realistic side of my identity knew different. This phone call couldn't have lasted more than thirty seconds but it succeeded in intensifying my frustration, why couldn't they just deal with my problem? Then, just as I was about to ring the bell again one of the nurses rode down on a wheelchair.

'Mr. Flynn, your chariot awaits.'

This was more like it, finally things were staring to move. I wanted to ask if there was anything I needed to bring, but I knew she would say something snappy like, 'only your ass' so I said nothing.

Into a wheelchair and off I was whisked, out of the ward and down the corridor. We hit ninety down the main straight, and then spun into the student facility at the other end of the hospital. A receptionist gave the nurse a little slip of paper and through the double doors we travelled.

'If you could take your robes off and lay on the bed over there, the class will be in shortly.'

I span round to clarify this but the nurse was gone, leaving me alone with an over active imagination and loose bowels. My dignity was unsafe again, the word 'class' indicated a headcount of ten plus, as well as a time duration of half an hour or more. I had complained and finally got what was coming to me, creating a scene wouldn't save me from punishment now. A doctor breezed into the room.

'Mr. Flynn, pleased to meet you I'm Dr. Lewis, thank-you so much for allowing us to film today's class. It's people like you that help the nurses of tomorrow.'

'Film?'

'Yes'

I wanted to tell him to take me back to the ward and leave me to rot until tomorrow but I had come this far and desperately wanted to go home. Okay, so a few male students would see the cheeks of my ass and that wasn't good, but the odds were that I'd never see them again. Mathematically, it was twenty-four hours of boredom divided by half an hour of humiliation equalling a quick exit.

In came the students, all of them females, all of them trainee nurses in those sweet little outfits that spark all manner of perversion. I lay on the bed my bare ass pointing upward towards the camera and begged God to make me invisible. It was all very succinct, they sat down, opened their books and prepared for notation, when everyone was settled the doctor tapped his pen on the desk.

'Ladies, I would like to introduce a fine supporter of our facility. Today, Mr. Flynn has agreed to be our model in what proves to be an ever popular form of exploration for stomach and back passage problems.'

I wasn't a hundred percent certain but I'm sure I recognised two of the students. They giggled and pointed and then I knew I was no longer anonymous. Dr. Lewis walked to the television screen and tapped the image of my ass.

'Basically, I will be working up here and you'll be able to watch my progress on the television screen at the back of the room. Girls, please don't forget to take notes.'

He coughed and cleared his throat.

'This is sometimes an uncomfortable scenario for the patient, so could I have a volunteer to come up here and talk to Mr. Flynn while we carry out the procedure.'

I knew what was coming and had accepted that this would be the worst day of my life. One of the girls who I recognised, a girl I'd been at college with, put her hand up and volunteered herself for the friendly chat as the doctor stabbed and pried my ass. What kind of conversation do you have with a nurse when your backside is being inspected by her colleagues? Surely we wouldn't engage in hairdresser chit-chat, 'you got a holiday booked this year?' I didn't want that, why couldn't they just leave me alone to fester in abashment?

Up she glided, as a woman she'd filled out in the two years since I'd seen her last. That was at college where she'd studied in the block next to me, then she was just a gawky girl with braces who I used to tease. Now she was something quite different, in her little white uniform she walked with all the confidence of a woman with revenge on her mind. Every joke that was used at the expense of her teeth two years ago was about to be paid back in the form of a really nice conversation during my anal examination.

'Hi Mike long time no see.'

The doctor talked on in the background unaware of the double torture.

'We understand you have a problem with your ass. What have you been doing with it?'

I winced as the camera hit a bend awkwardly.

'Oh that must have hurt a bit, do you want me to get the doctor to slap some more K-Y jelly up there?'

'Fuck off!' I hissed, 'Fuck off and leave me alone.'

She giggled and looked at my naked body.

I'm sorry I know how embarrassing this thing is, come on we'll talk about something else.'

Another joke was on its way, her revenge would only be complete when she had sustained a period of abuse on me.

'Let's talk about your small cock while we're here.'

For many years after this event I would often bump into these nurses at the most inappropriate of times. Sometimes on interviews and sometimes at work, and each time they saw me they would always heckle me with, 'Nice face shame about the ass!'

If there's any moral to this story, I suppose it's to be mindful of how and when you complain, remember the customer is *never* right, only unfortunate.

CHAPTER 9
Rescue

I needed you to salvage me.
Guidance on my shoulder's praising me,
Rocked, told 'everything's fine'.
Feasting off the child-like vine.
I'm unsure desired of answers.
Clear path his way,
Free of thorns and spines,
A map of mother time.

Christmas was something that I wasn't looking forward to, as tough as I pretended to be I knew that Christmas was going to throw up a lot of emotions, things that I'd managed to keep under control. I'd never had a Christmas like this before, a time of sadness and regret, from December onwards everything was painted black. Every advert I saw and carol I heard brought a lump to my throat as I stumbled over Christmases past where I'd been with people I considered my family and friends. You see Christmases with Karen had been almost magical events where *everything* was wrapped, and the presents you got were *always* the ones that you *really* wanted. People in Karen's family made a really big effort and would do everything they could to hype up the event some six weeks out from the 25th December, I knew I would miss this. It sounds terribly self indulgent but this year I would wake up in unfamiliar surroundings on my own, there would be no excitement, it would just be another day of the year for me. A few people asked me what I was doing and invited me along to their own family gatherings, they were all extremely sweet offers but not what I wanted. I knew that when Christmas day finally struck there was a good chance that I wouldn't be the most happy of persons to be around, I didn't want to be the pain in the arse that ruined everyone's Christmas. I wasn't without options though, I could spend it on my boat working, I could spend it at the Salvation Army or I could travel to Kent and spend it with my parents. Things between Karen and myself were good. She was moving forward and this made me happy, but in moving forward there were occurrences where I'd started to feel uncomfortable in her happiness. Early on in our separation she'd changed her surname back from Flynn to Treweek and for some reason this really upset me. It wasn't that I wanted to go back or anything, but changing her surname drew a bold line underneath our history together, it sort of said 'out with the old and in with the new', and here I was with another bridge burned. This insecurity was capped when she got a boyfriend in December, I wasn't sad and I wasn't happy, I just didn't care anymore, It was concluded. Over. But in being over it was as if we couldn't be friends anymore, we couldn't laugh together when we did we ran the risk of treading on someone else's toes. They never said anything but her parents didn't like us being together. I knew this because on their last holiday to America they had brought Karen back a voodoo doll in my incarnation.

    I feel guilty saying all these things because I really am glad she's happy, I never wanted her to dwell on our separation, but once again I'm having to deal with an ending. These are my weakness, these are the things that I'm no good at. I don't know why, really I don't, but I do know this. I can only enjoy the 'here and now' if I cut loose the past and make clear and defined endings in my life. If I continue to live in the past then guilt will always be my God.

As November came to a close and December broke I found myself dipping into the dark. Everywhere I went I heard the same songs, I couldn't even trudge the same streets without being bombarded with tinsel and happy reindeers on the tops of people's roofs, it was bloody awful. Things at the house had become more intense with the introduction of two rabbits as family pets. They lived in the conservatory where I usually had a smoke, now everytime I'd light up I'd have to wade through a million chocolate chips courtesy of the rabbits. Worse was the contemplation of smoking cannabis, if I dropped a round ball of dope on the floor I'd know I'd never be able to find it in all this shit. The landlady's daughter and the Bristolian's personalities began to unfold further with the introduction of two fish. These two couldn't handle the responsibility of getting up on time every morning, how were they going to cater for the life needs of another species?

I wasn't knocking the two girls because stepping back from pets for a second I could see that they were nothing more than surrogate children to their couples, these two were playing happy families. I was okay with this in theory until I realised that being the oldest member of the make believe family probably bestowed me the title of Grandfather or something. Then I became bitter and started thinking 'cheeky bitches'. I don't dislike animals or anything, I mean for a long time I've tried becoming a vegetarian, but much as I appreciated them, the rabbits stank. Not a little smell but a massive public loo stench and it was hardly surprising either, from the moment the rabbits woke to the moment they went to bed these two little bastards crapped their way through anything that even looked edible. This didn't matter to them though, the stuff that went in and out of the rabbits was completely ignored by the two little girls playing mother. In their fairytale sweetness they'd failed to remember that the excrement that passed through the rabbits exit holes would get underneath the tiles and then start to smell.

Bright days were the worst, when the sun hit the lean-to and heated the place up all sorts of things would depart. I didn't like this because the conservatory was my place, my little escape from the Bristolian who loved to bombard my life with stories about spotty teenagers she'd met. It was alright for them they didn't smoke, they didn't have to stand in that conservatory come rain wind or shine, I did. I daren't have one inside, they may have not been able to smell the rabbits, but bugger me! They could smell an roll up from half a mile away.

My First Saturday Job.

Your National Insurance card comes through the post and suddenly you feel all grown up. Instantly there's a host of things you want. Your Mother buying your clothes is now unacceptable as you beg steal and borrow to cover your loins in Calvin Klein or Tommy Hilfiger. This all costs money, a substance that teenagers often think grows on trees, so what did you do? You get a Saturday job. Saturday jobs are not just there as a source of income, Saturday jobs are an education, a rite of passage if you will.

My first job materialised at fourteen in Coxheath DIY shop just outside Maidstone, my bosses were a couple of simple fifty-something people who'd thrown everything they'd got into a little village business and then lived off the humble rewards. Life has many teachers and up until that point I'd never really had an understanding of the word 'focus', but after a few weeks with those two I understood the word back to front. You see, the business was not just a business it was a way of life, and Dave and Beryl were solid as rocks in giving nothing less that 110%. They worked seven days a week every week, always on call to a host of moneyed customers who saw Dave as the cure to everything that dripped or leaked. This was just the surface of it though, the cold reality of the Coxheath DIY shop was that the business was not based on hard work, but denial.

Dave and Beryl had a daughter called Elaine, a sweetheart of a child who'd filled their every waking moment with completeness. Only a little girl, but in the scale of things an extremely huge part of their lives. They'd never admit it but the birth of their daughter was emotional blessing. Dave and Beryl were tough industrious people and Elaine had added a gentleness to the hard exterior of their lives. People like Dave and Beryl were always on the go they needed to slow down, and Elaine helped them do that for the first eight years of her life. How were they to know that the blessing they had received could be taken away just as easily? I don't have children myself so I can't comment first hand, but I imagine having children is an extremely stressful occupation. New borns would be the worst for me because you can't communicate with them conventionally, if they have a pain they can't tell you about it. As they get older this obstacle is crossed as language develops but then other worries start to take over. Who are they hanging around with? Are they taking drugs? When Elaine reached eight these were the type of worries that Dave and Beryl were having, but all of this was about to change.

One day Elaine was sent home from school complaining of stomach pains, she was given pain killers and put to bed. The following morning she was dead. Appendicitis had taken this little angel from her parents. This is normally a rarity because appendicitis is a treatable condition, but in this instance Elaine had been misdiagnosed with Colic by a local GP. In twenty-four hours the whole framework of their lives had collapsed, they may have had each other but essentially they were both alone. Dave and Beryl couldn't cope so they bought a business and threw all of their time into it. Adoption and fostering had been denied to them because of their age, questions were thrown up around their ability to cope with a small child.

On my first day at the shop I was shown round all of the aisles and told that if I worked here I would have to learn where everything was. I was also taken to the workshop where the bags of cement were stored, and I was told that I would be expected to lift these into customer's cars. Finally I was shown to the kitchen where a broken teapot sat and told that this is where I'd make the refreshments.

'Do you have any questions for me?'

I wanted to ask how long my dinner break was, and I wanted to ask if I was allowed to use the toilet and I wanted to ask when home time was, but I didn't. I was on a three week probationary period one foot out of place and I'd be out. So I just smiled sweetly and said.

'No I think that covers everything, I'd like to start work now if I may.'

Dave adjusted his glasses it would take more that fancy words to impress him.

'Very well, load all the cement into the back of my van, and then make us all a cup of tea.'

There were twenty-five bags of cement weighing twenty-five kilo's a time, that was a total of six-hundred and twenty-five kilo's. The journey from the shop to the van was one-hundred and twelve feet each way, which was just under a mile in total. It took me two hours to complete the task at a payment rate of one sixty-five an hour, that worked out at roughly one pence for every five steps of pain. Everytime I passed the counter on the way to the van Dave laughed, making comments like I was 'slowing up' or 'looking ill'. Being ridiculed like this doesn't do much for the morale but at least I had a nice cup of tea to look forward to. What did it matter anyway, I only worked two days a week, he worked seven. I closed the van doors, the cement dust had taken the moisture from my mouth, but now it was time for tea and sandwiches-a real picnic.

Making the tea was no picnic, the pot leaked like a colander all over my hands and up my arms, burning with hot liquid as it went. From the looks of it the porcelain teapot was almost as old as Dave and Beryl probably with the same amount of holes too. I'm not moaning again because I love a cup of tea like the next person, but I associate the act of drinking tea as a relaxing pastime, and not one of risk. A few weeks of making the tea at this place and I'd have all the scars of a tribesman from Africa. I took the teas out to Dave and Beryl.

'What took you?' Dave snapped in his Scottish accent, I was quickly going off him, didn't he realise what value for money he was getting out of me?

'Sorry, the kettle was a bit slow.'

Dave looked up and frowned, something obviously designed to make me feel uncomfortable.

'A bad workman always blames his tools.'

He had a bloody answer for everything.

'And finish that tea quick, the plants are dying for a drink out the front of the shop.'

God, he made me mad! Didn't he see how hard I'd worked, didn't he see I'd earned fifteen minutes rest? I guess this was what my Father described as the 'real world'.

After drinking my tea as quickly as possible I watered the plants outside the front of the shop this took me round to twelve o' clock. Then I swept the cutting room floor, and made another cup of tea. (Burning my hands again in the process) At the grand time of 1.17pm. I was allowed to go to lunch. Dave obviously liked value for money from his staff, I mean, they did invent copper wire in Scotland didn't they? Two 'Jocks' arguing over a two pence piece.

Lunch back at my house was good, my Dad had cooked a massive breakfast, we were never rich in our house but we were always well fed. I sipped my tea, it was nice to relax amongst the less industrious members of the planet. Although successful in his own way I could never remember my Father working a seven day week, coming to think of it I can never remember him doing a seven day month. I don't see this as his fault though, my Father and Dave were people with different ideas. My Father was a 'here and now' person he like to deal with things as they arose, quite easy going preferring to rely on his wits and charm. Dave on the other hand liked to plan everything with military precision, if he couldn't see what was happening five years down the road he'd freak. Looking at it now I would have been invincible in the world of commerce if I'd been able to combine the wit of my Father with the industriousness of Dave.

'What's the job like Mick?'

My Dad asked, eager to know of his son's trip into 'adultdom.'

'Okay, but the Damn teapot leaks all over my hands.'

My Father laughed,

'Are you pouring it properly?'

'Of course I'm pouring it properly.'

My Father caved another road of toast and placed it under the grill. Other households had medicine, some had alcohol, but whenever we had problems it was always food.

'Well why don't you just ask for a new teapot?'

'*Dad*, my boss is Scottish.'

'Oh I see.'

I consumed another mouthful of food mindful of building my energy stores up.

'Well why don't you just drop the teapot on the floor, they'd have to get a new teapot then, wouldn't they?'

I stopped eating.

'What you mean drop it?'

'Of course I mean drop it! *And* break it! But make it look like an accident and that way you won't get into trouble.'

'It's a thought I suppose.'

And that's what it was, everytime I ventured into that dingy little kitchen and burnt my hands I thought. Thought about the tight Scotsman laughing at me, thought about my knuckles that were becoming warped under the heat, and thought about the new teapot I could have if only I dropped this one. I could have dealt with the pain if he hadn't drunk so much tea, but as long as he was drinking eight cups a day. the thought would always remain firmly planted in my mind. Then on one particularly wet day when everything was quiet in the shop I cracked. I liked the job and I liked the money, but I couldn't carry on with the leaking teapot. So at five fifteen just before I was due to finish work I took the teapot and threw it to the wind. The teapot sailed through the air majestically before meeting its fate with the ground, but it wasn't to explode in the way I wanted it to. Instead of breaking it twisted and bounced dispersing chips of clay as it went, I got worried and kicked the enchanted vessel, but the best I could manage was to break the handle off before Dave came bounding in.

'What the hell's going on here?'

I composed myself quickly.

'It's the teapot, it accidentally slipped out of my hands.'

I used the word, 'accidentally' thinking it would subliminally coerce Dave into dealing with me gently.

'Do you know we've had that teapot twelve years, twelve years and you manage to break it in four weeks.'

Dave got down on his hands and knees and picked up the pieces of the handle, I felt guilty because although he'd never said it, I knew that dilapidated teapot meant something.

'Go on get yourself home, the rains killed everything.'

I know it's inappropriate but as I turned the collar of my jacket up and made my way home, I smiled. Happy that my baby white fingers would now be safe from the one thing in the shop that threatened to transform them. Back home I couldn't wait to tell my Father who always appreciated a story about the working classes rising up and taking control.

'Dad I done it!'

'Done what?'

'I smashed the teapot.'

'Smashed' was a strong word, but when retelling a story it's always better to bolster it up a bit. If I'd used, 'dropped' or 'slipped' it wouldn't have had the same dramatic impact.

'Good for you.'

It wasn't good really, it was vandalism and now when I think of it I realise that all through my life I've always tried to prove myself to my Dad. I don't understand why, because my family life was never set up that way. My Father was never the type of person who'd crack the whip or taunt me to be something I wasn't, he was just my Dad. It took me to the grand old age of twenty-nine to realise that I wasn't him. I also realised that before I could make him proud of me I had to proud of myself. He smiled and patted my back.

'You see, there's always a way round these things.'

He was right, but surely the healthiest thing would have been to challenge Dave directly and not taken the matter into my own hands. Doing things this way stopped me holding my head up high. When I made my way to the little shop the following weekend I was apprehensive. I was frightened that I might be challenged about the situation further, and this fear didn't sit well with the person I wanted to be at the time. You see, teenagers create these larger than life personas that feed their self-esteems, but they don't realise that in creating these make believe characters they ultimately cause themselves problems.

That's why they're never understood by their parents, the parents still see the little child that they've moulded, but they don't see the people they're trying to become. I was never going to be my Father but I was still trying to do the type of things he'd find quick and funny. Psychologists will of course have a name for this, but to me it will always be childhood stupidity and waste, but I wasted twenty-nine years finding that out.

'You're late!' Beryl said, two minutes to be precise.

'You'd better make a cup of tea for Dave.'

I nodded and took my coat off, two minutes was hardly gross misconduct but to protest my innocence or to offer an excuse at this stage could upset the situation.

'Oh and Dave's got a surprise for you in the kitchen.'

'What kind of surprise?'

Beryl looked up from her newspaper.

'Go and see him.'

I surmised that she must be talking about the new teapot but I didn't like it, in my books the word 'surprise' had both positive and negative connotations. I strode carefully to the kitchen at the other end of the shop and walked in.

'Morning Dave.'

'You're late!'

Three minutes now, but I decided once again to bypass this type of conversation.

'Beryl tells me you've got a surprise for me.'

Dave smiled a miserly grin, no doubt the same grin Scrooge had used when counting his money at the end of the day. I was holding out for a new teapot but I began to feel the undercurrents of a new agenda unfold. Dave had his hands behind his back.

'Close your eyes and put your hands out.'

I closed my eyes but I was dubious because these were the type of things that homosexuals said when they decided to come out. I knew it wasn't going to be another teapot because I'd already broken one, and Dave being Dave wouldn't place another one in my hands without some kind of stern warning. I heard the rustle of a bag and then something made of fabric was placed into my hands.

'You can open them now.'

I opened one eye and then the next, unsure of what I was going to find, but after a seconds focus I knew what it was. Oven gloves! Dave picked up the old teapot with no handle.

'We just couldn't get rid of it, it was the last present Elaine ever bought us.'

Dave's eyes took on a distant look. I gulped. How could I have been so rotten? I wasn't cut out for a life of ducking and diving I had too much of a conscious. I needed something softer, something like nursing where I could save people everyday.

'If this one's so precious why don't you buy a new one?'

'Cost Michael!'

I hated this attitude, who the hell wanted to be the richest body in the graveyard?

'You're joking right?'

Dave's determined face was replaced with a look of discontentment.

'Michael, I can assure you I never joke around the topic of money. Anyway, at least you won't burn your hands anymore.'

He left the kitchen happy, and as they say in rugby, 'the referee's decision was final'.

I wanted to curse, and I wanted to tell him to poke his job but I couldn't, I needed the cash. I'd got to that age where girls were no longer satisfied with a quick snog they wanted to be taken out, and that cost money. So I kept my mouth shut, stopped listening to my Father, and ended up spending the happiest three years of my life as their Saturday boy. I learnt more about business from those two than I ever did from any course or mentor, God bless you Dave and Beryl.

CHAPTER 10
Home

Cramped like fish in a catchers net they gasp for air,
Swallowing the last sustenance before freedom.
Foreign waters they swam and sailed,
Little ships made of balsa and drawing pins.
Colouring the crests of waves,
Painting in the depths of blue with red.
From home to Eden and back,
It had all been a lie.
A filthy snatch of deception,
Where the streets were paved with gold,
And every man was born a millionaire.
All lies.
Returning home to familiar smells,
Mother's cooking and Father's flesh.
Returning home to familiar noise,
Dog's barking and children's mess.
The ticket is worn as a passport falsehood,
The money is gone all strewn on the land.
The heart has travelled but always belongs here,
My love of sea and my love of sand.

Christmas, and Answers

By the 20th December I was feeling tender, just about everybody had finished classes and most of them had made their individual ways home. I'll admit it, the first couple of days were nice, I appreciated the silence. Living in an environment that thrives on disturbance has it's own set of 'stressors' and being hidden from this made a nice change.

Normally I'd be okay with the quiet, I like the quiet, but it was different this time because I hadn't chosen the silence, the silence had been imposed on me. This was new ground and I was anxious with it. The stillness was so powerful that it had grown a persona and if I closed my eyes I could almost see it. A medieval like creature sitting in an alcove chanting 'nobody cares', it's funny what the mind can do when you're on your own.

By the morning of the twenty-third I was crawling the walls wishing I'd excepted all those nice invitations, the isolation had made me regress and all of a sudden I couldn't cope. I wanted to call Karen I really did, I knew she could save me, but I realised that it wasn't fair or healthy for either of us. She had her own life now with a new boyfriend and who was I to ruin this? I was feeling regretful because after everything we'd said to each other I now felt I didn't have the right to pick up the phone and ask for help anymore. To quell my black mood I went through a whole host of actions from chocolate to upbeat music, I called friends under the guise of humour, I even wrote some Christmas cards to people I didn't like. Nothing could make me smile.

I made a cup of tea, rolled a cigarette and sank down into the armchair. You know you've reached rock bottom when you turn the television on but keep the sound off. Luck or fate I don't know which but when I was at my lowest ebb the phone rang, it was my Mother. As a rule I don't open up to her often but this time I needed to spill and she was the closest thing I had to a counsellor. I freed my mouth and starting talking and by the end of it I couldn't stop. Most of what I said couldn't have made sense because I lunged verbally from one topic to another, but I hadn't spoken to anybody in three days. My open vulnerability was something she'd never seen before, and she was taken aback, I'd been erratic but never weak. She asked me to come home for

Christmas and I told her 'no', inside I wanted to say 'yes' but on some level I was content in my misery. After some emotional Ping-Pong she asked me again and this time I thought it wise to say 'yes' in case she didn't ask again. I was quite clear in what I wanted though, self indulgently I wanted to go home and be saved, I wanted to be held and I wanted to be listened to, all the things I thought I'd been starved of. On the telephone I was promised a relaxing environment with no stress but the reality was to materialise as something quite different.

From the moment I walked in to the moment I walked out on Christmas day I was hassled. Moved from A to B, shifted everytime I happened to get comfortable. No one asked after me, and I wasn't held in the way I wanted to be, all this made me hot under the collar. This wasn't my parent's fault I was sitting on so much anger that even the Pope would have annoyed me.

This rot started to set in hard on Christmas Eve after my sister had dropped me off at the one safe pub in Walderslade. I can't remember its name now, I think it's called the 'Windsor' but I can't be sure. Regardless of how safe it was, it will always stand as the most hostile place on Earth to me.

I entered the pub in my green students jacket complete with East German flag, took a crumpled wad of money from my pocked and stood at the bar. A barmaid, possibly the landlady caught my eye and made her way over to me, I smiled and pointed at the bottled beers, before I could speak she said,

'Tickets only.'

Cool.

'I'm sorry, did you say tickets only?'

'That's right tickets only.'

On Christmas Eve I was setting myself up for a fall but I couldn't help it.

'How much are the tickets?'

'Twenty pounds.'

That didn't sound bad, I'd probably spend that during the extended hours anyway, in fact being depressed gave me the right to shell out twenty pounds on booze.

'Okay I'll have a ticket.'

'Sorry we're sold out, you'll have to leave now.'

The barmaid was in the driving seat she had all the power, sure she could use her discretion and let me in but this was a woman with no Christmas spirit in her heart. She didn't give a toss that I was on my own, nor did she care that I might leave this pub in my depressed state and jump in front of a bus.

This was all about her rule book, her inadequate personality and the power she had as an ugly woman.

'I don't suppose there's any chance of one for the road?'

She leaned over the bar.

'No chance whatsoever, now please go before I have to call someone.'

It was a bit over the top and I felt strangely judged by this woman. I mean, I hadn't caused any trouble and I hadn't been rude, so why was she being so unfriendly to me? Didn't experience tell her that happy people tended *not* to drink on their own at Christmas? I buttoned my coat and left the same way I came in, only this time when I got outside it was raining cats and dogs, my Christmas cheer was now complete.

It took me an hour and a half to get home which was bad because it gave me ninety minutes contemplative time that I didn't need. When I got home Mum and Dad were watching TV, we spoke but they didn't really notice me going up to bed. I didn't do this for dramatic effect, I went to bed because if I stayed up I would end up crying in front of them. At 2am Penny came in from her boyfriends house or should I say ex-boyfriend, that right, true to tragic form Penny had managed to fall out with someone in this the most hallowed month of the calendar year. Downstairs I could hear raised voices but I lay perfectly still, if she knew I was awake then she might want her bed back.

I'd had a good cry through the night and the next morning (Christmas Day) I felt better. There was a time not so long ago when I never cried, but these days I seemed to do it all the time. Mum got up first and made us all a cup of tea, we didn't say a lot to each other because she could see I was still hurting. Since I opted out of the rat race and entered into full time education she didn't know what to say to me anymore. Her little boy had changed, and although his shape and size were the same he might as well have been a stranger standing in front of her, because she couldn't touch him in the same way anymore.

I called Karen and wished her a 'Merry Christmas', only a quick conversation because I knew she'd be busy, but nice all the same. It was one of those awkward things that you don't like doing but know you have to for peace of mind. I can't remember what we said to each other and it didn't matter, I just wanted to know that she was alright, and thank God she was. In a funny sort of way I found the telephone call calming, knowing she was okay gave me less to worry about. My Mum asked me how I was feeling and I told her 'hungry'.

We opened our presents and shared a giggle over Penny's latest break up, with Penny adding all the spiteful details in. She is funny, but she does pick them, half an hour of that and I started to feel ashamed of my gender, '*do we know what we are doing to these poor girls minds?*' We watched television, we ate dinner, we pulled crackers, we drank tea. I couldn't be here anymore, no one was annoying me barring me, but the claustrophobia was killing. Fuck I hate Christmas.

I slung my coat on and went for a walk, and somewhere up on the waste ground in Walderslade village I found a climbing frame. No one was about so I climbed to the top and had a look around. I used to play on these things when I was a kid, I was always a King or General, never a Sergeant. I used to play with weaker kids so they'd never complain about me being the leader all the time, and it was a system that worked well for me. If history could have been recorded it would have shown that I was an abysmal leader. I'd always send my troops in on rescue missions with zero chances of success, and quests, quests of no commercial value to the Kingdom. My success was all about righting wrongs, revenge, justice, I never constructed anything I just stopped things being built. My desire for leadership came out of the belief that everything in the world was wrong and that only I was right. Of course I'm not stupid, I know the odds of me being totally right and the rest of the world being totally wrong are quite remote, but I didn't know it then. That was the problem, I had always strode to be in charge but never should have been given the opportunity to do so. I felt too much, and this feeling would cloud my judgement and turn me into a Maverick. Someone like Robin Hood who robbed the rich to feed the poor, the trouble is, heroes like this have a short life span. I mean, who wants to be married to someone like me? 'A hero without a cause'. I became a leader because I wanted admiration, and that love of admiration was fuelled by my inadequate feelings. Bad leaders have to hide behind something and my shield was words. I always knew what to say and how to act, the difference was I never believed in anything I ever said or done. I never woke up in the morning and thought 'great'. And I think that's the difference between people who've found it and those who haven't. I think the first fifteen minutes of any day is the truth, the reality. Your room is cold because you don't control the heating, breakfast is crap because you can't afford anything more than toast, and you've got holes in your shoes. This is life, but I can do one of two things, I can like it and look at the things I have got, or I can lump it and continue to go under. I may not like where I am, but I can enjoy where I'm going. I can celebrate the man I nearly am and not the man I was.

Splitting up with someone is not something I advise, but like other bad things in life it happens, even adults fall out of love sometimes. What you're not prepared for are the other things it brings up, those little insecurities that you've so cleverly hidden in the back of your mind. Contrary to popular belief, divorce is not a liberating experience. The whole thing from beginning to end has just made me sad, more importantly made me question everything about myself. Who am I? Where am

I? Why did I marry Karen? What did we do wrong? I'm fed up feeling guilty for everything and I've decided not to do it anymore. To see this metamorphosis through, to be myself, to be happy, to be content, I have to get right back to the beginning and attain zero. I've had so many personas over the years that I'd simply forgotten who Michael Flynn is. In my previous life I always knew what I was doing at least two years down the road, one of the most stressful things about my predicament is, that more often than not I don't know what I'm doing tomorrow. I'm going to be okay with that now, I'm going to except that I can't control everything in my life. I'm also going to except 'me', I'm hereby giving myself permission to be upset when I feel down, to laugh when I'm feel happy and to finally be at peace with my separation. I'm going to do this by being myself. When I get down off this climbing frame and my feet touch the damp dirt I'm going to stand up straight. Not crocked and unconfident, but proud that I've come out the other side.

    On the way home I felt baptised, clean, holy. As a person I thought I was nothing more than a collection of short stories but now I've learnt that I'm much more than that.